One Life Stand

J.B. STEPHENS

Interior Formatting: J.B. Stephens

Cover Design: Megan Jayne Designs

Editing: Bianca Shakur

Paperback ISBN: 979-8-9950501-1-7

Ebook ISBN: 979-8-9950501-2-4

Disclaimer

The author does not condone some of the actions that occur in this book. This book is intended for a mature audience and is strictly for recreational pleasure. It contains content that may be triggering, such as sex, profanity, death of a parent, and a potential step brother x step sister relationship.

Jamaican Creole is used for some narrations. There is a glossary in the back matter with contextual translations.

For more about the author and her books, visit: authorjbstephens.com

Chapter One

WHERE THERE'S A CRUISE, DON'T GET THROWN OVERBOARD

Rhyan

I didn't hate many things in life, but this all-inclusive cruise was surely working its way to the top of the list. Earlier today was the last of the two-day stay in Kingston, Jamaica. It was nighttime now, and the bartender was being such an asshole about giving me another drink.

"Come on," I begged, glancing from the white male bartender to the empty shot glass on the counter before me. "*Please.*"

"Ma'am, you are at your limit," he explained with that same sickeningly sweet smile that was doing nothing but making my mood more sour. "Our rules state three drinks per patron."

"All I've had were shots," I pressed. "Three, to be exact. So I should at least get three more to make up for them not being full glasses."

"Ma'am."

"I get it," I said, and he smiled again before walking away to shine glasses that were already sparklingly clean. I huffed and propped my elbow on the counter. I rested my head in my hand while moving my tongue around my mouth, savoring the remnant flavor of the best espresso martini shot I'd ever had.

I wouldn't say I was a caffeine addict, but the damn thing just kept calling my name whenever I was on the road or at home.

Okay, *fine*. Maybe I was a bit addicted, but this time, that was beside the point. The cruise ship left the Kingston port a few hours ago, and there was no other way for me to get my fix until I was back in Jacksonville, Florida.

With the cruise line having a last minute change with my cabin and issuing me an inner room with a faulty shower faucet, I felt like this was the least they could do for my troubles, especially because I was really looking forward to the room on the higher deck with a balcony, but I digressed.

"I'm sorry," came a voice from my right, and I stopped adjusting the plain black headscarf wrapped around my dyed honey blonde curls to see a handsome man looking at me like I was the first woman he'd ever seen.

At five-foot-eight, I could be considered a tall girl, yet I could tell that this man would still tower over me if I was standing. He was maybe six-foot-three, with skin as dark as chocolate, and a perfect white teeth smile. His goatee and mustache combo, plus his full head of waves complimented him well. He was dressed simply in a white tee and dark jeans, gold studs in his ears, and a gold watch around his wrist. Him looking that good with minimal effort made me feel overdressed at this time of the night in my mini dress, silver hoop earrings, and more silver around my neck, wrists, and ankles.

I stopped gawking just enough to recover. "Sorry?" I repeated.

"I saw you from across the room and came to say you're beautiful, but that's an understatement. Please accept my apology," he said, his voice smooth and deep.

I chuckled. "That's new," I mused. I stopped fusing with my scarf to cross my arms one atop the other on the bar. "Thank you."

"You're welcome," he said, then glanced at the bartender before looking back at me. "Hey, I also overheard your conversation with the bartender. I have a bottle back in my room. Want to come with?"

I pursed my lips together as I continued to watch his hopeful expression. Was I so desperate for a fix of *something* to wash my worries away, that I was here seriously contemplating following a strange man back to his room?

Why, yes.

Yes, I was.

"Sure," I replied, and he perked up even more.

I grabbed my purse off the top of the bar and hopped off the stool. Now closer to the man, I caught a waft of his scent — something spicy and woody. It activated a switch in my brain. One that hadn't been flipped as yet because enough alcohol wasn't in my system.

That'd change soon enough.

The bartender glanced at me, torn as he looked between this handsome stranger and me. I discreetly flipped him off before allowing the stranger to guide the way.

He didn't speak to me at all as I trailed one step behind him, to which I was thankful. I got to admire him more from the back, plus keep one eye open just in case someone jumped out of a corner and grabbed me. With a man as fine as this, it would either be a partner in crime or a woman who didn't play about the third leg he had in his pants.

I halted.

The stranger looked over his shoulder, raised a brow, then stopped walking, too. "You good?" he asked.

I awkwardly chuckled. "Of course," I rushed out. "I thought I heard something," I added, not knowing how to tell him that my mind had gone somewhere that it definitely shouldn't have.

I mean, sure, he was very tall. But from my experience, tall men either had a third leg or a matchstick. He couldn't blame me for wondering.

"Okay," he said, then waited for me to take the first step before he continued leading us through the hallways. A moment later, he stopped before a door. "Wait here."

I nodded and watched as he disappeared into the cabin. I smiled at the cracked door, thankful he hadn't tried to invite me in. Maybe he really only wanted to drink and didn't have any sinister intentions.

He came out of the room with a bottle tucked into a small bag. He closed the door behind himself and motioned his head for me to follow him. He took us to a spot that had minimal foot traffic compared to other areas of the large cruise ship.

"Wow," I said as I sat on one of the chairs at a small round table. "At first, I thought you would've tried to keep me at your cabin."

He chuckled. The rumble came from deep within his chest. "Nah."

"You're careful. I like that."

"One of us has to be," he said as he unscrewed the bottle and I heard the seal break.

"It's not careful if you're offering a strange woman a drink."

He pushed the bottle across the table towards me. I caught it with my hands, but I didn't move to take a sip. His eyes had a playful glint in it as he said, "It's careful enough."

"How about you take a sip first?" I pushed the bottle back toward him.

He chuckled again. "Being careful now?"

"You won't be tossing me overboard."

He stopped reaching for the bottle. His brows pulled together as he looked at me, genuine confusion washing away the playfulness from moments before. "I'd never do anything like that."

"Drink," I urged as I placed my purse on the table.

He stared at me for a moment longer. I shuffled about the chair. I couldn't help but realize that by making him uncomfortable, I'd managed to do the same to myself, too. His stare was too intense.

Scrutinizing.

Unsettling.

I could barely breathe as he watched me and held my stare. It made me notice everything about his appearance all over again. It made me realize how well his spicy, woodsy scent blended with my warmth of vanilla and jasmine. It made me wonder what his name was, but I wouldn't dare to ask. This was the first cruise I'd ever been on, and I'd learned early on in an effort to fit in, that many people weren't on a first name basis with each other.

Cruises were meant to be an escape. Being someone else for a few nights — a person with no name, or a person with a different name every night, or a person with no connection to whoever they actually were back in America.

Oxygen flooded my lungs as soon as he finally looked away. He tilted his head back and held the bottle in the air to pour some of the clear liquid into his mouth. He lowered the bottle back to the table with a grimace while wiping the back of his other hand across his mouth.

"Satisfied?" he asked.

I grinned. "Very." I took the bottle and did a waterfall, too. The Wray and Nephew White Overproof Rum burned going down, but I welcomed the taste. As I put the bottle in the middle of the table, I asked, "How did you find this spot? It's so quiet compared to the rest of the ship."

"My dad called me one night and my room was too far away. I stumbled into this spot while heading there," he said.

"Must have been an important call."

He shrugged and leaned back into the chair. He crossed one arm over the other. "As important as him telling me he's about to have his fifth wife and wants me to be the ring bearer... Again. Some calls lose importance over time," he explained, and my eyes widened. "Don't give me that look."

"I-I-" I stuttered, searching for an answer that could mask my surprise, but I couldn't come up with any.

Fifth wife? This man's father was something. Was it a sign of mental illness or of a person who lived a daring life? I wasn't sure, but I was still stupefied either way.

"Guess he just hasn't learned his lesson since the first four. It's hard parenting parents, right?" the handsome stranger joked, dispelling the awkward air that had settled around us.

I released a short laugh and rolled my eyes. "I can tell you all about it," I said, and took another waterfall from the bottle.

Shit. What was this? I pulled the bottle back and read the label. My eyes bulged.

Sixty-three percent?!

This thing was strong enough to make me meet my maker tonight. But it was lessening my headache as it lowered my inhibitions. Who was I to complain?

The man chuckled at my reaction as he held his hand out for it as I was putting it back on the table. My breath caught in my throat as I looked from his hand to his eyes.

There it was again.

That intense stare.

Captivating.

Gripping.

Making my heart race because this wasn't supposed to be happening with a man I didn't know. Wow, the alcohol really was moving fast.

I forced myself to breathe. My near nonexistent chest rose and fell at a quick pace. I wetted my lips, and his eyes followed the action. I nervously chuckled. "What?"

"Go on," he said, taking the bottle from me. "Tell me."

I dragged my hand from the table and laid it in my lap, joining the other. My hands balled into fists as soon as they settled. "At least ask for my name before I start unloading my traumas onto you," I said, hoping he knew the trace of anger in my tone wasn't directed at him.

He grinned, showing me those straight, pearly whites that seemed to glow against his dark skin in the dimly lit area. "What's your name, beautiful?"

"Guess it," I dared. "I bet you never will."

"Hmm..." he hummed. As he trailed off, he took another sip from the bottle, and his eyes raked over me.

Goosebumps raised all over my skin from his attention. I resisted the urge to shiver, but my body just couldn't help it. My nipples were very reactive, straining against the material of my dress as they hardened. Now, I was really starting to regret not wearing my pasties. The discomfort of religiously wearing a bra had never made sense with my B cups.

A smirk came on his lips as he placed the bottle back on the table. He could tell his undivided attention was having effects on me that it shouldn't have, but he saved my dignity by not mentioning it.

"You're wearing a necklace," he noted. "Unless that 'R' stands for a boyfriend I don't see near, your name starts with an 'R'."

I winced and relaxed my fists. "I don't look like I'd have a husband?" I asked, slightly offended.

He shrugged. "Unless you chose not to wear your ring tonight, there'd be a tan line around your finger — but that's not there, either."

I gasped. "Tan line? I'm not that light skinned!"

He chuckled. "You are, beautiful."

My eyes pressed together in a playful glare. I reached across the table for his hand. I pressed them together, trying to compare the shades of our skin, but instead I noticed how small my hand was compared to his. How rough.

I didn't like touching hands. They carried so many germs, and my high schoolers taught me that well. Remembering this fact, I got a hold of myself and dropped his hand.

"Point proven," he said with a grin, but I couldn't tell if he was asking or telling me.

I rolled my eyes. "You win this time, mister…"

"Kingston," he said. "Kingston Badalo."

I almost laughed. Meeting Mr. Kingston when we were in Kingston a few hours ago? Oh, the irony. I guessed he was the type to give fake names on a cruise.

"Whoa," I said, choosing to play along. "Never knew we were doing full government names."

"You don't know that though. Isn't the purpose of cruises to be someone else for one week?"

"True," I agreed, nodding profusely.

"Who do you want to be, Miss R?"

"Rhyan," I answered. The Rhyan before my shit show of a life went up in more flames a few months ago.

Kingston's brow raised. "You want to be a man?"

I mimicked his actions. "Never met a girl with a unisex name before?"

"I've met Robyns. Never met a Rhyan."

I looked around. "You've met my mom?"

She was the type who would sneak onto the cruise with me. Of all the things she'd done throughout the twenty-three years I'd had the on-and-off pleasure of knowing her, this would've been fighting for a top spot of the most infuriating things she'd done.

"Rhyan and Robyn… Interesting," Kingston said.

"Says the person named after the place we just visited?" I asked, my brow raised.

"In my defense, all my siblings and I are named after where our dad met our moms," he said. "What's your excuse?"

A smile came onto my face. "It goes back as far as my great-grandmother. Her parents wanted a boy, but got her instead. Since then, it's been a tradition to give the girls a unisex name," I explained, surprising myself by how at ease I was with this man. I reached for the bottle again, put it to my lips, and took a large chug. My throat stung as it washed down, giving me the fuel to say my next words, "I no longer feel like you're trying to throw me overboard, so— Wait," I paused, and he raised a brow, watching me with curiosity while I hooked onto all of his minor movements. "Do you have a girlfriend?"

His Adam's Apple bobbed. "Not at the moment."

My eyes narrowed on him, and he gulped again. "Not a straightforward answer."

"We can be anyone we want to be for tonight, right?" he asked. That charming smile came back onto his face, but it wasn't enough to distract my mind from the question I'd asked.

But it did manage to rid the absurd thought I'd almost breathed life into. My resume wasn't impressive beyond being a high school counselor, and I'd never dare to add home wrecker to it.

I pushed my chair back and stood. The smile wiped off his face. He stood, too.

"Well, nevermind, then," I said, looking anywhere else except at him. I found intrigue in the nearby railing and pondered if I should just do us both the justice by throwing my own self overboard. How could I be so foolish to come back here with this man, knowing that too much alcohol always made my clit develop its own heartbeat? "I don't want to be in the middle of the breakup of a happy house."

"I live in an apartment."

I snapped my head around, settling my gaze on him with a ferocious glare. "Kingston."

He wetted his bottom lip. I couldn't tear my gaze away as his pink tongue trailed across his just as pink bottom lip. My mouth parted slightly.

"My name sounds good coming from your mouth," he said, and my heart skipped a beat. "Well?"

I dragged my gaze to his eyes. There was that hope again. That intrigue. Those naughty thoughts that shouldn't have been returning to plague my mind.

"You said you don't have a girlfriend?"

He nodded once. "At the moment."

I exhaled a shaky breath, unable to believe I was about to go through with this. "I never want to see you again after tonight. I'm already mad at myself for considering this, but I..."

"You're horny, and I'm irresistible," he finished.

I dryly laughed and reached for the bottle and my purse off the table. "My room or yours?"

"Yours," Kingston said. "My apartment only has one room."

"Not funny," I said as he led us away from the quiet spot. I felt guilty knowing that I liked having him walking beside me, his shoulder grazing my arm every so often.

"It was," he disagreed, and I looked up at him to see him grinning down at me. "Admit it."

I rolled my eyes and looked ahead of me. I couldn't let him see that I was smiling at his lame joke. He had this warmth and joy to him. I hated to admit that I liked how attractive it made him, but maybe that was just the alcohol talking. One thing was certain though — whoever his 'not at the moment' girlfriend was, she was one lucky woman.

"The only thing I'll be laughing at is if your big talk doesn't match what's in your pants," I said, finally able to lead the way to my room.

Chapter Two

WHERE THERE'S A FIRST IMPRESSION, SHOW UP... PLEASE.

Rhyan

I yanked my large framed shades off my face and gave the waiting area by the docks another once over. Clearly, I must've been blind, because why was I still yet to see my mother?

This woman was going to drive me up a wall.

Grumbling, I fixed my glasses back onto my face before shifting all of my attention to my phone. I found her contact and dialed it. She answered after the phone rang a few times.

"Mom?" I said, unable to keep the edge out of my voice.

"Hi, bestie!" she greeted.

I bit into my tongue to stop the words that almost slipped from my mouth. "Where are you?" I asked instead, and her end of the line went deathly silent. I exhaled a loud, long, heavy breath through my nostrils.

"Oh, baby, I'm so sorry," she said. "I forgot that you were coming back today. I'm still at yoga, but I can get there soon."

"How soon, Mom?"

Uncertainty laced every syllable of her words as she said, "An hour?"

"I'll call you back, Mom." I ended the call before she could get another word in. I didn't want to hear anything else she had to say. It would probably be more excuses, and frankly, I was far beyond the point of simply being tired of them.

All of my money was tied up in other expenses at the moment, and I didn't want to put myself into more debt by calling a cab. Capitalism and its interest fees be damned.

I debated whether I wanted to scroll through my contacts to see if anyone would be kind enough to give me a ride home. The whole reason I'd wanted Mom to come for me was because I knew she would do it out of the kindness of her heart for her one and only child, but now I'd likely have to pitch in on gas.

"Thanks for nothing, Mom," I complained as I opened the contacts app. My thumb froze above the name at the very top of the list — Adaejah. She was my gorgeous, dark-skinned best friend, who I met in college and formed a tight bond with over our mutual disdain for group projects.

Unfortunately, I didn't want to be around her either. We weren't on the best of terms at the moment, but she'd never leave me hanging.

Sighing in defeat, I rang her cell. She answered almost immediately.

"I'm really sorry to bother you, and I know we weren't on good terms when I left," I began, and she sighed, knowing that I was coming with my bullshit. "But I called you to ask for a favor."

"Go on," Addie said.

"Could you come pick me up? I'm still without a car. Mom was supposed to come pick me up, but—"

"I can be there in thirty minutes."

There was my girl.

I breathed a sigh of relief. Sure, we were at each other's throats every now and then, but I didn't know what I would do without her.

"Thank you so much, Addie! I owe you."

"You don't," she disagreed, then hung up.

A broad smile popped up on my face — showing all my thirty-twos and bright enough to combat the sun. Oh, if Addie were here right now, I'd kiss her!

I was just about to pocket my phone when a new text message popped up from my mother. The message was censored. My phone needed to be unlocked for any new notification to be read. My high schoolers were curious little things who stuck to me like I was their Mommas, so I had to draw boundaries somewhere.

I scowled at the notification and chose not to even read her message. Though

I had to admit that a part of me was curious, I wouldn't feed into it.

My good mood had plummeted to zero, and I needed a tall cup of coffee to reignite my shine. I looked around the port, still scowling while I read the names of the shops across the street. Spotting a restaurant, I squealed, took my luggage into my hands, and dashed across the street.

KINGSTON

As I closed the trunk of the rental car, a person on the other side of the parking lot caught my attention. I'd spent only one night with her — fucking, sucking, doing all things sweet, unholy, and everything in between — but I'd know Rhyan Fagan anywhere. That pretty, slim thing had her curly hair tied up in a fancy updo with a multi-colored scarf. She was dressed more simply compared to last night. She was in a tank top, perfect for the Florida heat, and some skinny jeans with sandals.

How could she look so beautiful with such little effort?

A part of me wondered if she'd intentionally done that.

If she'd just known we would've seen each other again, and she wanted to still look good for me.

I was about to give her another once over when I realized something was a miss. Where was her captivating smile from last night? Rhyan had the meanest scowl on her face. One I didn't know a gentle soul like hers could muster.

Worry pinched at my heart, making it race while I suddenly found it hard to breathe. I was overcome with the urge to march over, put a smile on her face, and do cruel things to whoever had dared to make her this angry.

We'd sworn that our interaction was only for one night, but how could she expect to put that bomb, grippy pussy on me and not expect me to feel a semblance of possession over her?

I was about to walk over and do anything to put a smile back on her face when she squealed out of nowhere. My brows pulled together as I watched a smile appear on her face. I wondered if she had mental issues, and I meant that with no disrespect. From my experience, women with good pussy were never truly right in the head.

Rhyan grabbed her luggage and bolted across the street to the strip mall that my sister, who lived here in Florida, had told me was constructed recently. As she disappeared into a restaurant, a switch went off in my head, and I came to my senses immediately.

I wasn't the type to break the boundaries of women. Rhyan and I had agreed on one night, and I shouldn't disrespect her by driving across the road, finding her in that restaurant, and demanding her number.

Besides, she probably had a boyfriend, anyway. I refused to believe that a shorty like her was single.

I sighed. "Nice knowing you," I said, giving the restaurant a final look before I walked to the driver's side of the car. I hopped in the vehicle I'd rented and connected my phone to the radio. I blasted the latest Dancehall songs as I made my way to the airport. I wasn't prepared for what was waiting for me back home in Newark, New Jersey, but I had a real life to get back to.

One without pity cruises.

One without Rhyan.

I rubbed my eyes as I walked into my apartment. I kicked the door shut with my foot while tiny footsteps hurried towards my direction. A smile came onto my face as my baby ran up to me. The handle of my suitcase fell from my hand as I kneeled to her height. "Skye," I drawled, laughing as I rubbed her all over.

She was a small, tan and brown bundle of energy as she jumped around and barked. Her tail wagged and her tongue hung out the side of her mouth.

"I missed you too, girl." I patted and rubbed the Yorkshire Terrier's head, feeling the pink bow loosely tied around her fur in a ponytail brush against my palm. That sunken feeling in my chest returned with a vengeance, but I couldn't force it away even as I stood and moved away from the door. Skye ran around my feet as I headed to my bedroom in the high-rise apartment and began stripping from my clothes while calling my boss.

"Oh, brother," Timothy answered, then heavily sighed.

I chuckled. Tim was a whole fool. This man was pushing sixty, yet his personality hadn't changed since I'd known him. If my dad were a lanky white man with a salt and pepper beard, he would've been Tim.

"Can I pick up a shift?" I asked, and Tim sighed loud and heavy again as if I was his teenage son who'd just come to him and said I'd already outgrown the shoes he bought for me last week.

With the long history Tim and I had, I might have well been his son. We met when I was in high school and was eager to make a little money on the side. My dad already gave me everything, but there'd definitely been times when I loved having money without having to ask my old man for it. Tim hired me right on the spot at this fancy ass restaurant called Escargot on a more fancy side of New Jersey, desperate for a busboy because one of his employees quit on him suddenly.

As a kid, I wasn't complaining about the type of job. I went there every day with the biggest smile and left with an even bigger grin every time I got my cheque. I worked my way up from busboy to kitchen aid to the second head charcutier. It got to the point where I wasn't only working at Escargot for the money, but also for the experience. A lot of influential people came and went from there. Escargot and the employees, especially Tim, taught me many skills and truths about life long before my old man got around to doing so.

"No, Acheem," Tim said, dragging me from my thoughts by using my middle name, which only those close to me called me. "You know the answer is no."

I frowned. "What's the reason?"

"*Reason*?" he repeated, aghast. "Acheem, you're on vacation. *Vay-cay-tion*. Do you need me to spell it out for you?"

"No," I answered, glancing at Skye as she rolled around on the floor while playing with a squeaky toy ball. "But I know the restaurant's probably busy. Let me come in. If it's even for a few hours."

Tim sighed. "I wish other twenty-six-year-olds were as hardworking as you, but I've got to decline you, kid. You have to learn to take a break sometimes."

I almost scoffed at the irony. If Tim knew what a break was, Escargot wouldn't have expanded beyond New Jersey. It wouldn't have a catering company that did charcuterie for small events.

"How can I learn what a break is when my mentor never takes one?"

"Don't start with me, kid. Rest. I mean it. You deserve it. I'll see you in a month, or I'll call you if we're swamped with events that need catering, alright?"

I sighed. "Alright."

Tim hung up. I tossed my phone onto the bed. There went my desperation for a distraction from this aching hole in my chest.

I looked around my room, picking at my brain for things I could do.

I could unpack my suitcase. I could go shower. I could go on an angry fit and destroy every piece of furniture in this room that reminded me of the woman I was so desperately trying to forget.

"Fuck!" I cursed, annoyed that my room still smelled like her.

I needed to burn the silk sheets on the bed.

I needed to change the bow in Skye's head.

I needed to erase every memory I had with that woman who had my whole heart in her hand and drained it of everything I had to offer. There was no more blood left in my veins. If anyone put a knife to my skin and made a long, deep, cut, there would be no blood.

My jaws clenched tight, and I moved to the ensuite bathroom. Maybe a long shower could do the trick. The warm water trailed down my skin as I stood below the stream. I held my head down, enjoying the feel of the warmth in my hair.

After my shower, I returned to my room and got dressed in casual clothing. I headed back to the living area, about to take Skye for a bathroom break because I wasn't sure how long she'd been here. Though she was potty trained, she had her times when she was a little brat like her mother, and would search the entire apartment for the hardest corner to clean, just so she could piss in it.

As I reached for her leash hanging off a hook close to the door, my phone rang from within my pocket. I fished it out. I read the caller ID before answering.

"You're back," said my old man.

"Yeah. So you can log out of my doorbell camera now," I said, and he chuckled.

"No gratitude for me getting my friend to take care of your dog?"

"Thanks, Daddy," I said, smirking.

He sucked his teeth. "Me tell you don' call me Daddy. Me name Marvyn. Daddy a fi batty man, and if me was a batty man, me wouldn' have you or the ungrateful one dem," he said, a thick Jamaican accent replacing his usual American one.

"You can't take a joke, Marvyn?" I teased, laughing.

"No. I can't." He sucked his teeth again. "I'd called you to tell you that I'm glad that you're back, but I don't feel like it anymore."

"Right," I said sarcastically, and he chuckled.

"I really am, though. I was getting tired of this co-parenting situation that you got going on — which is nonsense, by the way."

My grip tightened around the phone. "What's the real reason for your call, Marvyn?" I asked, glancing at Skye, who was impatiently scratching at the door.

"My trip down south," Marvyn said. "It'd make a great impression if you came with me."

I sighed. I'd been so caught up on that cruise, trying to forget the whole reason I was on it in the first place, that I'd forgotten almost everything about Marvyn's newest engagement. The conversation hadn't even held my interest when he'd been telling me about it. Marvyn fell in love with someone new damn near every month, so I didn't exactly care if one of them finally stuck around for long enough to be called my step-mom. Still, I'd played the role of a good son by gracing him with the occasional nod and hum.

Ready for the conversation to end, I grabbed Skye's leash and attached it to her bedazzled collar. "I'm coming to the wedding," I said to Marvyn. "Isn't that enough already?"

"Acheem..." Marvyn said, and I stopped reaching for the door. He rarely called any of his three children by our names. On the rare occasions he happened to be around two or more of us, he always just spoke and expected us to already know which one of us he was talking to. "Please. Do this for me."

How could I tell my old man no when he was practically begging me? I guessed this time he really was serious about Miss Whatever-Her-Name-Was, who he met on his trip to Las Vegas.

"I'll be there, Marvyn," I promised and ended the call.

Chapter Three

WHERE THERE'S A HEADACHE, LOSE THE HEADSCARF

KINGSTON

Skye sprinted from one end of the fence to the next. She sniffed at the blades of grass, huffed, then ran to the next spot.

"Any day now, Skye," I said, and she ignored me as she did another sprint. Amused, I shook my head while watching her. We were at the back of the apartment complex where I lived, the moon fighting to peek out of the clouds as the sun descended and Newark remained awake.

My pocket vibrated. I swapped the poop waste bag to my next hand so I could dig in my pocket for the phone. Once I pulled it out and saw the caller ID, I froze. My jaw clenched tight. Boiling anger coursed through my veins as the phone continued to vibrate in my palm.

Against better judgment, I answered the call, but remained quiet.

"Acheem?" she said. The tenderness in her voice broke my heart all over again.

I lowered my head and closed my eyes, trying to push away the resurfacing feelings, but all I saw were the memories of her with another man.

My teeth were grinding hard against each other now, threatening to break each other apart. I lifted my head, my eyes following Skye, as I forced myself to answer, "Nataliya."

"You're back."

I looked around the empty backyard, my brows furrowing. "Are you stalking me again?"

"N-no," she said. "Not exactly."

I sighed. "Nataliya, I told you to stop this."

"I just saw that Skye's tracker was in the backyard. I know Marvyn's friend wouldn't walk her all the way back there," she rushed out.

I wasn't moved by her words. I scowled. "What do you want?"

"I miss you," she sobbed. "I miss us. It was a mistake, and—"

I yanked the phone from my ear. My fingers fumbled over each other as I hurried to end the call. My breathing was heavy as I stared at the blank screen.

Nataliya had no right to cry in my ear. How could she be so cold? I wasn't the one who ruined our almost three-year relationship. She didn't deserve to be the one who was hurting. Cheating was never a mistake. We were all grown adults. Unless Greg had forced her to drop her panties and get fucked over her work desk, Nataliya knew what the fuck she was doing.

My lips twisted into a scowl. "Skye!" I shouted, and her head snapped up. "Let's go," I said. Her mom pissed me off, and I had enough of her being undecided on if she wanted to piss, shit, or both. She ran over to me, and as we walked back to the front of the apartment, I couldn't stop my mind from wandering to Rhyan.

As sure of myself as I'd seemed on that cruise, I was actually the opposite. I'd been on a few cruises, so I didn't lie when I said they were great for pretending to be someone else. A part of me wished I could've kept up the farce with Rhyan for more than one night. We'd be more than the perfect strangers, laughing while we fucked, cuddling after we fucked, sharing some of our deep, dark secrets before we fell asleep in each other's arms.

I'd left her room after I got up in the middle of the night to use the restroom. It was hard untangling her limbs from mine, and even harder closing her cabin's door, knowing that I'd never see her again, and that I'd have to return to my new reality of dealing with the knowledge that my on-and-off girlfriend cheating on me hurt more than I ever expected it to. I'd done lots of shit to hurt her in our relationship, but I would've never stooped so low to cheat.

My problem in the relationship with Nataliya was that I never made enough time for her. She always complained that I worked too much, and I knew that was true. After our last big argument and temporary breakup about it, I promised I'd do better. I used up a chunk of my PTO — much to Tim's surprise and delight — and booked Nataliya and me a cruise to my father's homeland. After everything for the trip was finalized, I bought a bouquet of her favorite flowers to surprise her at work, but she surprised me instead.

It hurt now to even think about it. I could still imagine her legs over Greg's shoulder.

Her moans.

Her nails that I paid for, dragging across his shirt and making it crumpled.

What had made matters even worse was that it was too late for me to get a refund on the tickets. Ultimately, I grudgingly decided to go on with my cruise, and I gave the other ticket to Marvyn. Since I was a kid, he always told me that there was an opportunity in every disappointment, so I knew he'd find a better use for the ticket over me planning to discard it along with the memories and life that I shared with Nataliya.

The latter wasn't as easy as I'd hoped, but I was determined to stick to the plan anyway.

RHYAN

I moved my steaming hot mug of black coffee to my mouth. I looked over the rim of the mug at Addie, who watched me expectantly.

"Now that you've had your coffee in you, I think it's time we talked," she said, and I groaned.

I'd been blowing her off since last night, saying I was too tired to properly recount the events of my cruise, plus address our argument.

"Rhyan," she said.

"Addie," I replied, giving her a cheeky smile.

She glared at me from her position on the sofa in my living room. "Come on!

Tell me."

I sighed and pushed myself off the kitchen counter. I went to the connecting living room and made myself comfortable on the other end of the sofa Addie sat on. From this position, I could see into my bedroom. My queen-size bed was still a mess from sleeping like a log last night. My luggage was on the floor before my bed, clothes strewn everywhere from me searching for my favorite headscarf to sleep in.

Turned out, I'd been so tired after returning to the comfort of my own apartment that I hadn't realized the scarf was already on my head. I'd probably still be sleeping if Addie hadn't returned to my apartment at the ass crack of the day, cooked breakfast, and forced me to get out of bed by laughing obnoxiously loud as she watched reruns of her favorite show on my television.

"Well," I began, then cleared my throat. "What do you want to talk about first?"

"Let's start with Robyn," Addie said. "You shouldn't let her career define you like that."

I rolled my eyes and rested my mug on the nearby table. I crossed my legs over each other while carefully pondering my next words. "Then what should I do? It's like she's made it her whole life's purpose to make me ashamed of and embarrassed by her."

"Was it embarrassing too when she raised you on her own after your dad passed?"

My mouth dropped, and I bolted upright. "You know that's not what I meant!" I exclaimed, but Addie wasn't moved. "I meant that she's too old to be doing the stuff that she does. I shouldn't be at school hearing my students gossip about my thirty-nine-year-old mom's half-naked pictures in magazines when she should be looking forward to her retirement in less than a year."

"She's a lingerie model. You keep leaving that part out," Addie defended.

"Whatever," I huffed, rolling my eyes and crossing my arms as I looked away. I pretended to be interested in the show on the television, hating that Addie was on Mom's side instead of mine. I couldn't believe that we'd been on bad terms over this.

Was she Mom's best friend or mine?

Addie should've felt lucky that she worked at a different high school and didn't have to bear witness to what had become my daily torment.

My parents had me young. They didn't make that deter them from being amazing parents. Being raised by teen parents was fun until it just... wasn't.

They both had a whole plan to take care of me. During the four years Dad worked full time, Mom stayed with me. Despite being a very active Mom, she spent a lot of her time at the gym, getting her body right for when it was her turn to do her four years. Their plan was for Dad to care for me until Mom was back, then he'd reenlist to do another sixteen years. They had all their 'T's crossed and all of their 'I's dotted, prepared to make full use of their joint benefits to shame anyone who ever dared to open their mouth and say they wouldn't do well as teen parents.

But they never got to prove anyone wrong.

Just as Mom was to enlist, our lives took a turn for the worse.

Dad never came home.

Mom lost herself.

I lived with my maternal granny, Riley, until she passed too, and Mom had no choice but to take me back into her life. Turned out, during our time apart, a dark industry preyed on the toned body Mom built to serve this country. Over the years, I did my best to ignore different types of print media out of fear of seeing her on a cover.

That all changed recently.

Apparently, older women were all the rave now, and Mom's career was booming more than it ever was before.

With a shake of my head, I sighed. I reached for my mug, but Addie beat me to it. She grabbed the mug and placed it atop the table beside her side of the sofa, far out of my reach.

"You've had enough caffeine for one day."

"This is only my second cup for the day!" I said defensively. I'd drank my first cup through mouthfuls of the egg sandwich Addie made for me. This mug was for me to savor until the very last drop.

"Addict," Addie laughed. "Tell me about your trip!"

Kingston popped up in the front of my mind. His dark complexion. His pearly whites. The smoothness of his groomed hair. The soft hair in his goatee. The veins in his dick. The curl in his toes as I rode him in reverse cowgirl.

I blushed and looked down at my lap.

"Ouu!" Addie teased, and I dared to look at her. She wiggled her brows at me, making it harder for me to hide my blush. "Girl, you're flaming red. Did you find a door with one of those upside-down pineapples on it?"

"What?" I laughed, willing my heart to stop pacing while I reminisced about Kingston.

A dumbfounded expression came on Addie's face. "You're not being serious, are you?"

"As a heart attack." I stood from the sofa and walked around it to grab my mug. I took a sip and looked down at Addie, who watched me closely. "What does that mean?"

"Oh, you young grasshopper," she said, then waved me off. "Never mind that for now. Tell me about the cruise."

I blushed again. "I hooked up with a guy. Nothing serious."

"Yet he has you turning into a tomato?" Addie teased. "Tell me about it."

"Okay, okay!" I gave in, already excited to relive last night's events, if even through memories. I was about to return to my position on the sofa when the doorbell rang. When it didn't stop after a few seconds, I sighed.

Only one person would press the doorbell for seconds on end, refusing to be ignored.

I placed my mug back onto the table and answered the door. An older version of my face greeted me, with a darker complexion and eyes that held none of the annoyance that shone in mine.

"Bestie!" she said, reaching up to throw her arms around my shoulders. She yanked me down to her height of five-foot-four and engulfed me in a tight hug. Some of the black strands of her curly hair went into my mouth.

I spat out her hair and hesitantly patted her back. "Hi, Mom."

She pulled back with the biggest smile still on her face. She walked further into the house and gasped. "Oh, hi, Addie! I didn't know that you were over here. Thank you so much for getting Rhyan yesterday."

Addie smiled while she stood to accept Mom's hug. "Of course, Robyn. It was no problem at all. It's nice to see you," Addie said as they broke from the hug. As Mom made herself comfortable on the sofa, Addie grabbed her bag and tossed it over her shoulder. She approached me, still disgruntled at the open door. She pulled me into a hug and whispered, "Be kind to her. She's your mom."

I sighed and closed my eyes briefly. "I'll see you later, Addie." I pulled away with a tight-lipped smile, and she nodded before walking through the door. I stood in the doorframe, watching as she walked to her car. Whenever I didn't have noisy upstairs neighbors, I loved living on the bottom floor. I always got to easily watch my guests make it safely to their cars before I went back inside my apartment.

I grabbed my mug and moved to the kitchen. I drained its contents into the sink, my appetite gone, and began washing up the dishes.

"Bestie, guess what?" Mom asked.

"*Daughter*," I corrected with a roll of my eyes.

Without looking over my shoulder, I knew she was frowning as she replied, "You used to love that name when you were little."

"Exactly. When I was little. I'm a grown woman now." I turned down the last item to air dry, then wiped my hands on a towel. I turned around and leaned against the sink while crossing my arms across my chest. "What do you want, Mom?"

"I'm getting married!"

My eyes bulged out of my head.

My mouth dropped to the floor.

My heart stopped beating for a few moments, causing my chest to tighten in a reminder that I should breathe.

I sucked in a shaky breath and barely managed to force out, "M-married?" The word tasted foreign on my tongue. I couldn't believe what I'd heard.

I knew death freed a living spouse from a marriage, but a part of me felt betrayed for Dad. How could Mom be moving on?

Anger shrouded me.

My body grew hot.

Staring at her bright eyes and large smile made me truly notice her for the first time since I'd been showing up to my job embarrassed. She hadn't looked this full of life in years. This excited. This version of Robyn Fagan that I loved because she was my mom, rock, supporter, and everything all in one.

My bestie.

There was a large rock on her finger. It glistened beneath the early morning sunlight streaming through the blinds over my window into my living room.

I loosened my fists, which I hadn't realized had tightened. I was torn as I moved over to sit beside her. Slowly, I took her hand into mine. Inspecting the band from every angle made my throat tighten.

I hated that the ring fitted her slender finger well.

I hated that it wasn't Dad's ring.

I hated myself for wanting her to be happy, but not if it meant she'd finally move on from Dad.

"Is this real?" I asked, my voice low.

"Of course, it is!" She snatched her hand out of my hold. She held her hand up to the light, making the glimmer almost blind me. "It's pretty, isn't it?"

"Who are you getting married to?" I asked, unable to keep the bitterness out of my voice. "Last time I checked, you weren't in a serious relationship. And that's before I went away on my cruise."

"Well, life moves fast."

"Mom, who is he?"

"He's an investor."

My brow raised. "What industry?"

Mom sighed loudly. "Jeez, Rhyan!" she exclaimed, lowering her hand to her lap and glaring at me. "I came over to share my joy with you, not play twenty-one questions. Besides, I thought you would've been happy because I gave you a proper vacation. I thought you looked stressed and needed a break before you went back to work."

I gasped and prodded beneath my eyes with my fingertips. "I looked stressed?"

"Bestie, the bags beneath your eyes could hold the entire Atlantic Basin."

I dryly laughed. "Funny, Mom," I said, and she grinned. I crossed my legs over each other and rested my hands on my knees before redirecting the conversation. "Where did you meet him?"

Mom pouted. "You're not happy for me, Rhyan. Why do you always try to ruin my mood lately?"

A heavy sigh passed my lips. I pinched the space between my brows as I looked away. She was giving me a headache. I loosened the scarf in my hair, making the honey blonde ringlets fall around my face. I needed a strong drink and another orgasm. I could hardly wait for her to leave so I could go put in overtime with my trusty vibrating dildo.

Realizing the quicker I got this conversation over with, the sooner she would leave, made me find some peace. I turned the television off and gave her all my attention. "Fine," I said. "Tell me about him."

Mom pursed her lips. "Hmph. Maybe another time when I know you're not doing this just because," she said. She mimicked my position on the sofa. Instead of resting her hands on her knees like I did, she propped an arm on the headrest and laid her head on it. "Tell me about your cruise."

I smiled. "It was great, Mom. Thank you. I really needed it."

She grinned. "Great! I'm so happy that you enjoyed it..."

My brow raised as she trailed off. "What is it, Mom?"

"I'm just wondering if now's a good time to tell you that he got the ticket."

"Your... fiancé?" I asked, and she nodded with an even larger grin. Yeah, I definitely needed that drink now. "Okay, Mom. Tell me all about him since you're so determined to," I said, and she began going on and on about the man. Her words came through one ear and went out the other as I went to the kitchen and poured myself a large glass of wine. As I made myself comfortable on the sofa again, I almost spat out my first sip. "What did you say?"

"Which part? About our meeting or how he's the first man I feel sure about since Jayden?"

I would've stiffened at the mention of Dad's name if I hadn't already become so tense. "No," I said. "His name. You said his name."

"Marvyn Badalo."

"Wow. Interesting," I said, finally allowing myself to relax. I thought I'd heard something completely different.

"How so?" Mom asked as she reached for the glass of red wine I'd poured her.

"It's my second time hearing that name in the past week. What are the odds?"

"Really?" Mom laughed, and I nodded. "So, you see, the thing about that ticket is... Marvyn gifted it to me. He told me his son's girlfriend cheated on him, but he didn't want the ticket to go to waste, so he gave it to Marvyn to give away. He's probably the one you met. His name's Kingston, but—"

I choked on the wine, coughing it up everywhere. Mom's eyes widened, and she yanked the glass from me, resting it atop the table while she rubbed my back.

"Are you okay?" she asked as I continued choking while disgust, shock, and so many emotions so hard to name, made my gut uneasy.

I shook my head in response, unable to find my voice because bitterness made my tongue heavy. Not because that unforgettable moment on the cruise was a rebound fuck, but because I'd had sex with my future step-brother.

Chapter Four

WHERE THERE'S A CAR, LEARN THAT THERE ARE LEVELS TO BEING A PASSENGER PRINCESS

Rhyan

I twirled the pen around my fingers while staring at the wall. I was seated behind my desk, a stack of papers before me.

The semester just started, and I already had a bunch of my students trying to change their pathway. I wasn't surprised that they did; I went through this with them every year. Before school went off for summer break, I'd pulled all my kids out of class, one-by-one, and discussed their futures with them as freshmen in high school. I guessed they did some reevaluation over the summer break, but I wasn't expecting it to be so many of them.

I wanted to go through these as quickly as possible so my kids could get their class transfers early in the semester, but I hadn't been able to focus like I'd like since I clocked in this morning.

I'd been on edge since Mom's revelations yesterday. And, to make matters worse, she and her soon-to-be husband had already gone ahead and planned a dinner for all of us to meet each other formally.

Kingston and I were going to be in the same room again.

"No way!" came a surprised yelp from the other side of my office.

"Let me see!" came another voice.

I huffed loudly and pushed my chair back to stand. I went to my door and opened it, my eyes searching the waiting area to find the students who were speaking so loudly. Some kids hung out in the counselors' office during their free periods, and us counselors didn't have a problem with it — so long as they used their inside voices. Them being here where we could keep our eyes on them was better than them roaming about the school doing God knows what...

Like totaling my car.

My teeth ground together at the memory.

"There she is!" came a whispered-yell, and my head snapped in the direction of a group of boys.

I walked over to them, and they all hurried to open their closed textbooks, just so they could pretend they were doing something.

"Boys," I said to them. "You know this is a quiet area. What's the commotion for?"

"We're sorry, Miss Fagan," said one of them, and I nodded.

"Just please keep it down," I reminded them before I turned on my heels and began walking back to my office.

"I told you that it was her mom," one of them whispered, and I froze.

Embarrassment consumed me. My skin became red as I willed the office floor to open up, swallow me, and only spit me out when Mom found a job that didn't require her to be half-naked.

Reminding myself that they were kids and I couldn't snap at them for being gossips about public information, I was about to pretend I didn't hear them and return to my office when a student came to my defense.

"Stop bothering Miss Fagan, jit. I know where you live," she hissed at them.

The corner of my mouth ticked with the urge to smile as I heard the boys leave the office. Remembering I needed to be the adult in the situation, I kept my expression passive as I turned around.

I easily spotted Zayria sitting in another corner with one of her friends. She was a sweet girl with a big personality. She used to play third base on the softball team for a year, back when I was its assistant coach and the school funded all sports equally, instead of only pouring into the football team.

"Thank you, Zayria," I said. "But there's really no need to come to my defense."

She shrugged. "I didn't mind it."

"I know," I said. "But I also know how teenage boys can be. I don't want you to get picked on."

As her friend laughed, Zayria smirked. "Miss Fagan, I have a big brother with big... utilities. They can't mess with me. I'm not scared of them."

My heart sank as I thought of a student who visited me earlier this morning. Tears were in her eyes throughout the entire session. She'd lost her dad to gun violence over the break and wasn't sure how she'd make it through the semester.

"For the sake of the both of us, I'm going to pretend I didn't hear that. Have a good rest of your day, ladies," I said, to which they smiled. I returned to my office and fully closed the door this time. I had a lot of work to get done. Unless it was my boss or one of my kids, I didn't want to be bothered for the rest of the day.

A loud, frustrated sigh escaped me as I yanked yet another formal dress off my body and tossed it to the side. My room was a mess. Addie was on the phone giving me more suggestions, but nothing seemed to give me the right vibe that I was going for.

I was already tired from work earlier today, and I didn't have time for this. I didn't want to go to the dinner — I didn't have it in me to face Kingston again. But I had to do this for Mom.

I wanted to look great because first impressions always mattered. I wanted something that complemented my body well in a subtle, sexy way, but I knew that was just my memories from Jamaica with Kingston talking.

"Addie," I groaned, turning away from the mirror to grab my phone off the pillows I had propped up against my bed. "Help me."

"I'm trying," Addie said, her brows pinched together, just as frustrated as me.

I sat on my bed, rested an elbow on my thigh, then propped up my arm to rest my head in my hand. "I don't know why I want to look good, anyway. I should just grab a trash bag and cut three new holes in it."

Addie screamed in laughter. "Rhyan! Can you be serious for once in your life?"

she asked, and I chuckled despite my dilemma. As Addie's laughter died off, she gave me a suggestive look.

"No," I said and tossed the phone aside before getting to my feet. "Don't go there again," I warned as I began rummaging through clothes on the ground and in my closet, desperate for something nice to wear.

"I can't help it," Addie said. "Your one-night stand is about to be your brother."

"*Step*-brother," I corrected, as if it was much of a difference.

"Exactly!" Addie agreed, making me stiffen at the realization that she'd baited me. "I could understand if you two knew about each other before you had sex, but you didn't. Besides, you're two grown adults, you aren't in a hurry to have kids, and it doesn't sound like he's looking for anything permanent right now. I don't think there's anything wrong with you guys having a little fun with each other."

I mulled over her words. I didn't like the idea of being used to get over his cheating ex, but that was just Addie giving me wild assumptions to steer my mind in the direction I was trying so hard not to let it go. But Addie and my conscience were right — Kingston wasn't my blood brother, we didn't know about our parents before we fucked, and we were both mature enough to handle sex with no strings... I hoped.

A brilliant idea went off in my head, and I raced back to the phone to grab it. "Addie, I'll call you later," I told her before hanging up. I found some casual clothes in the mess that I made, shrugged them on, then went out the door on a mission to the mall.

Mom's soon-to-be husband had chosen a fancy ass restaurant on the outskirts of the town I lived in, causing me damn near a leg and an arm to get a taxi here. I grumbled at the hole growing in my bank account as I stared up at the one-storey building with brick walls and dim lighting peeking through the arch-style windows.

A place like this was usually out of my budget. It quelled my worries about being overdressed in my simple yet elegant brown dress. The dark color complemented my skin tone well, and it had two skinny straps draped over my shoulders. Having titties the size of a cookie bite made me debate if I should wear a bra or not. Ultimately, I decided on wearing pasties, scared of how my nipples would react to being in Kingston's presence.

Gulping hard to wash away the nervousness and forbidden thoughts that popped in my head, I finally reached my hand out to cling to the railing. I watched my step as I mounted the three stairs, not wanting to break my ankles in these shoes. Heels weren't something I wore often. They were uncomfortable and made me walk awkwardly, but I tried my best to not make it so obvious as I approached the hostess stand.

The hostess greeted me with a warm smile and asked if I had reservations. I gave her Marvyn's name. As she was leading me to the table, I spotted Mom at a table by herself, sipping from a glass of water. Her face brightened as she saw me, and she put her glass down to wave.

My chest tightened. It became so hard to breathe all of a sudden.

"Excuse me," I said to the hostess, and she stopped walking. "Where's the restroom?"

"Right over there," she said and pointed to a corner.

I thanked her with a smile before speedwalking away. In the restroom, I dashed into a stall and pressed my back against it. My chest was caving in. My breathing was heavy and labored.

Was I seriously about to have a panic attack?

God, please. No.

I tucked my clutch between my thighs instead of resting it atop the toilet, then I bent over while fanning my face. *Breathe, Rhyan*, I told myself in my mind. *Who hasn't watched their parent move on before? Who hasn't fucked their step-brother before?*

My chest grew tighter. I patted my face, feeling its warmth beneath my palm.

"Calm down," I told myself. I stopped patting my face to rub my hand along my left arm. I could trace every line of my full sleeve tattoo by memory. I'd gotten it in honor of my parents, who loved tattoos but never got any because they knew their bodies had to remain within regulations. It was a montage with some of my most fond memories with them. My favorite was the drawing of them holding my hands, swinging me between their bodies as we strolled along a beach. The intricate details took me into their color and safely tucked me away into the safe space in my mind.

Here I was with Dad.

Here I was with Mom.

Here we were together.

My breathing evened out. The haze lifted from my being, and the world came back into focus around me.

I allowed myself a few more seconds to regain myself before I exited the stall. I moved to the sink and washed my hands while checking my face. I hadn't worn any make-up outside of mascara and a little lipstick, but now I wished I had. My skin was still slightly red from the surge of emotions, and I hoped it would even out by the time I returned to the table.

I exited the restroom. As I walked down the hallway, I bumped into a man who was walking with his head down. His wallet and phone fell from his hand, scattering all of their contents. We rushed out apologies to each other as we stooped to gather his things.

I gathered an array of different cards and handed them to him. "I'm sorry," I said again.

"It's no problem," he said, chuckling while tucking another set of cards into his wallet. "I need to pay more attention."

"Enjoy the rest of your evening," I said to him before I stepped around him and went back to the table. I hugged Mom before I took a seat around the four-seater round table. We were the only ones here. "Where's Marvyn and King— his son?"

"I'm not sure where Acheem is," Mom answered. "Marvyn should be outside taking a business call."

"Okay," I said.

She smiled and reached a hand across the table to lay it atop mine. "I really appreciate you being here, Rhyan. It means so much to me. Thank you."

There was that smile again.

The one that lit up every part of her face and made me want to freeze this moment in time so I could treasure it forever.

"You're welcome, Mom," I said, returning the smile. My smile gradually faded as a man approached our table.

He was dressed in a black suit, had a salt-and-pepper beard and hair, and he looked so much like his son that I wondered how I hadn't seen the resemblance when we'd bumped into each other by the restrooms.

"Ah, you must be Rhyan," Marvyn said.

A wave of discomfort rushed through me at how he said my name. It just didn't sit right with my spirit to hear my name on his tongue. I wasn't sure where this foreboding feeling came from or why it dug such a deep hole in my gut, but I put on my best smile as I stood to accept Mom's fiancé's hug.

"Marvyn," I said, a shiver running through me as he wrapped his arms around me. "It's so nice to meet you."

"The pleasure's all mine," he said before breaking the hug.

As we took our seats, Mom smiled brightly at us.

Guilt consumed me again. How could I be having such a bad feeling about this man without even knowing him? Was it because I'd fucked his son? Was it because I never wanted Mom to be with another man if he wasn't Dad? Was it because he'd put a smile on Mom's face that I'd tried for years but never managed to bring her back to that level again?

I needed to be an adult and give this man a chance. If not for myself, then for Mom.

"So, Rhyan," Marvyn said, dragging my focus from Mom. "Robyn tells me that you enjoyed your cruise."

"I-I did," I said with a nervous laugh. "Thank you."

Marvyn smiled. "My son was on the cruise as well. I'm not sure if you met him."

"I think she did," Mom said. "She mentioned meeting a Kingston."

As Marvyn hummed, I asked as casually as I could, "Where is he?" I reached for my glass of water and my eyes searched the restaurant while Marvyn answered.

"I'm not sure," he admitted, his voice tight as more warning bells rang in my head that I quickly silenced. "I'd given him a call when I went to the restroom, and he'd said he'd be here soon."

I hummed while placing the glass back on the table. A part of me wanted him to come, not just to see how amazing I looked after he dubbed me his rebound fuck, but just to prove to myself that I'd worn these pasties for no reason because my body would not have a raging, hormonal reaction to seeing that man.

"We can give him a few more moments to show up, or we can just go ahead and order," Marvyn added.

"I don't mind waiting," Mom said, looking from Marvyn to me. "How about you, Rhyan?"

I didn't mind waiting either, but frankly, I hadn't eaten since I came home from work. I'd been holding my hunger to leave enough space for this dinner. "I'd prefer if we began," I said. "Sorry. I just had a long day at work and—"

"It's fine, bestie," Mom said, and she called over our server to take our orders. After he left, Mom said to me, "I hope it doesn't take too long. I don't want you getting more slim than you are."

I chuckled. "Mom, I inherited those genes from you," I said, my eyes drifting to Marvyn. "How do you feel about that, by the way?"

His brows furrowed. "Pardon?"

"Mom's job," I said, and Mom's smile faded.

"Rhyan," she said sternly.

Marvyn placed a hand on Mom's hand on the table. He gave it a gentle squeeze. "It's fine, baby," he said, making bile rise up my throat. I grabbed my glass of water and gulped it down like my life depended on it while Marvyn answered me, "What about her job?"

I placed the glass back down. "Well, we both know that Mom has her job because she looks pretty amazing for her age. Will you have a problem with what she does?" I asked, hoping that he did. Maybe if Mom wouldn't listen to me about finding another career path, she'd listen to her soon-to-be husband. I was sure that no investor wanted their wife to be half naked on magazines for the entire world to see. Which reminded me that I needed to ask him about what he invested in. I added that to the list that I'd mentally compiled to vet if this man was good enough for my mom.

"Why would I?" he asked. "Robyn was honest about her career when we met in Vegas. Besides, she's hoping to retire soon. She told me that she's been saving up her portions of the posthumous compensation and she hopes to retire soon."

I stiffened. My mouth gaped, and I looked at Mom. She kept her gaze averted.

How could she tell this man, who was practically a stranger, about Dad's benefits?

My jaw clenched tight. Colorful words landed on the tip of my tongue, and I bit into my cheeks to not voice them. At the end of the day, she was still my mother, and I would rather get a boob job before I fixed my lips to disrespect her.

"I make enough money to maintain her," Marvyn added. "With or without those veterans' cheques. With or without her career."

"What kind of investor are you?"

"In simple terms, I invest in start-ups. Mostly those I see potential for quick growth and significant returns in, such as formal dining restaurants in white collar areas, and courier forwards to the Caribbean."

"Hmm. And you've told her about your four other marriages?" I asked.

Mom gasped. "Rhyan, that's enough—"

"It's okay," Marvyn assured her again. "You're protective of your Mom, understandably so. To answer your question, yes, I have. I've withheld nothing from her, and her, me."

My lips twisted into a sneer, and I moved the glass back to my lips to hide it. I hated that this man was ticking off all the boxes. His charm was undeniable, and his brilliance was evident in his speech. I could see why she had fallen for him so quickly.

I continued my interrogation of Marvyn over medium well steak, green beans, loaded potatoes, and a bottle of red wine.

By the time everyone was outside, saying our final goodbyes, Kingston still hadn't shown up. I wasn't sure if I was supposed to feel happy or disappointed.

"I'm really sorry he didn't come," Marvyn said, glancing between me and

Mom. "I don't want to make excuses for him, but he works a lot and might not have been able to travel from Jersey in time."

"It's fine. There'll be plenty more opportunities for us all to get together before the wedding," Mom said.

"Yeah," I agreed. "It was nice meeting you, Marvyn. Please take care of my Mom."

"I will," Marvyn promised with a nod.

I smiled at him, then hugged Mom. "Goodnight," I told them.

"See the bwoy deh!" Marvyn exclaimed, happy.

My brows furrowed as I looked at Marvyn. When he told me that he was originally from Jamaica, I hadn't believed him a bit. He had a very strong New Jersey accent, so it was equally surprising to hear how strong his accent could be when he spoke Jamaican Patois.

Still hugging Mom, I looked over my shoulder. A white sedan was parked a few feet away at the curb. As the front door opened and a tall, handsome man exited in his black tux and brown tie, I stiffened.

"Kingston," I whispered in disbelief.

There he was.

Alive in the flesh.

Very much the man I threatened not to throw me overboard on our cruise. Very much the man I fucked. Very much my future step brother. Very much the man who made me grateful for nipple pasties.

I pulled away from Mom as Kingston approached us. His eyes were wider than mine.

"Rhyan," he said in disbelief as he stopped before us. He stuttered out something inaudible before shaking his head. He reached a hand out for mine. "It's so nice to see you again."

"Likewise," I forced out as I placed my hand in his. I stiffened and pressed my thighs together as he leaned forward to place a chaste kiss on the back of my hand.

Why would he do this to me in front of our parents?

My heart raced a mile per second, and my eyes darted to my right to see our parents watching us, none the wiser.

Kingston released my hand. I instantly missed his touch as he greeted Mom and kissed the back of her hand too. "I'm so sorry for being late," he apologized. "I had some stuff I had to deal with in Jersey, ended up missing my flight, and I had to drive here."

"I understand," Mom said.

"How about I make it up to all of you?" he said, his eyes drifting to mine. My breath hitched at the look he was giving me. Gone was the surprise. It was replaced by a feeling I knew all too well, but was hesitant to acknowledge. "I can make you dinner tomorrow night?"

"I'm sure the ladies would love that," Marvyn said.

Kingston looked at his father. "Dad—"

"*Marvyn*. Wah'm to yu?" he grumbled, and Kingston chuckled.

"I'm sorry for being late," he told Marvyn, who grumbled again.

"Rhyan," Mom said, and I somehow managed to tear my gaze away from the man who'd captured all of my attention despite barely trying. "Do you need us to drop you home?"

I shook my head. "There's a coffee shop somewhere around here. I might go have a cup then call a taxi home."

"I'll ensure she gets home safely," Kingston told her.

My heart started racing, and I rushed out, "No—"

"Don't be silly, Rhyan. Let him accompany you and get to know each other better," Mom said.

"We know each other very well," Kingston said.

I choked. Mom rushed forward to help me in any way she could, but I assured her through a forced smile that I was fine. She gave me another once over before returning to Marvyn's side, unable to see me glaring at Kingston, who flashed me a smile that made me feel things between my thighs that I was ashamed to experience in the presence of my mother.

Mom and Marvyn left us. Kingston faced me and opened his mouth. I turned away from him and began walking toward the direction I remembered seeing the coffee shop in. One thing I loved most about myself was that before I tried a new restaurant, I always looked it up online first, plus checked out places in the surrounding area just in case I didn't like the food options from the initial restaurant.

"Rhyan, come in the car!" Kingston yelled at my back, and I pretended not to hear him as I continued walking.

As his car pulled up at my feet, trailing beside me and causing disgruntled drivers to honk their horns before going around Kingston's vehicle, I sighed heavily. I was starting to truly regret my decision to wear heels.

"Rhyan," Kingston begged again. "Please."

"No, thank you," I hissed.

He sighed. "Why not?"

I stopped walking and faced his car. I crossed my arms below my barely existent boobs, and his eyes flickered to them briefly before finding my heated stare again. "Because you knew about this. About *them*. Yet, you still had sex with me."

Kingston had the audacity to roll his eyes at me. "We had sex with each other. It was hardly a single effort with how much we were both coming that night."

I gasped. His candid words sent a throb right between my thighs and made my nipples harden some more. "How can you be okay with this?" I asked, desperate for him to give an answer that wouldn't make me wholly disgusted with myself for still feeling the things that I felt for him.

"What do you mean? We're adults, aren't we?"

"Yes..." I trailed off with a sigh. "But our parents are together, so that makes you my step-brother, and this conversation shouldn't be happening."

Kingston hummed. "I see how this can be wrong, but I also see how it can be right."

"R-Right?"

He nodded. "What other reason would there be for us to meet each other again?"

No reasons came to my mind.

Gosh. I hated myself for the taboo things plaguing my mind. I didn't think wine or coffee could save me at this moment.

Defeated by the realization, I continued the walk. The coffee store was coming into view. I hurried my walk to get away from Kingston.

A bell rang over my head as I entered the establishment. Spare a few late night patrons tapping away at their laptops or chatting with the person sitting across from them, the quaint shop was a ghost town. A soothing instrumental was playing at a low volume from speakers hidden somewhere. Freshly baked pastries on display within the cashier stand drew me close to the lady behind the stand who seemed around my age.

I ordered my drink and was about to pay for it when the bell went off again. On instinct, I looked over my shoulder. Should I lie and say that I was surprised to see Kingston Badalo? Because I honestly wasn't.

My eyes refused to leave him as he walked further into the establishment. He stopped by the counter, took a peek at the POS, then withdrew his wallet and tapped his card against the reader.

"Thank you," I told him with a small smile. Sure, I should've been vehemently insisting that I could pay for my own drink, but I happened to like it when men spent their money on me. Especially now, when I was in a rough patch with the sudden debt from my car. I'd never dare to touch Dad's benefits to get myself a new car, because I was already planning on using them to either get a house or go for my Master's.

"You're welcome," Kingston replied before we walked toward the door. He opened it for me and winked. "Ladies first."

My skin turned red from the sexually charged innuendo. I hurried out of the coffee shop like someone was threatening to rip my pasties off so the entire world could bear witness to my shame.

"So," Kingston said as we stood outside. "Should I drive you back to the restaurant so you can get your car?"

I sighed after my first sip of bitter goodness. "I don't have one right now."

His brow raised. "What happened?"

"Some kids crashed into it."

"One of your students?"

Now *that* was something I could never lie about being surprised by. "Wow," I said. "You were listening when I said I work at a high school."

He grinned. "Why wouldn't I?"

I shrugged. "And, yes, but they're not any of my students. They're seniors who were flexing the car they rented for Prom, and they ran into my parked car. The money I got as compensation isn't enough to buy a new car, and I'm past the age of getting a beater car," I explained, and he smiled. My brows furrowed. "Why are you smiling at my complaints?"

"Because you're already so comfortable telling me your problems," he said. "How can you fight this?"

I rolled my eyes and took a sip from my drink. "Whatever, Kingston."

He nodded his head toward the nearby car park. "Let me drop you home."

"I don't want you to know where I live."

He sighed heavily, a clear sign of his frustration. "I know about the large mole you have on your lower back. This is nothing."

My mouth dropped. Bewildered, I looked around, hoping no one had overheard him, but there was no one standing before the shop except us. "Shut up!" I hissed as I looked at him, and he laughed.

"Well?" he asked after his laughter died down. "Besides, our parents say we should get to know each other better."

Realizing he wasn't going to drop this, I sighed. After pondering for a moment, I came up with a brilliant idea. "How about you come over one day for a sip and paint?"

"Not my typical style, but sure."

I smiled. "Where's your car?"

The frustration left his eyes, replaced by the upbeat man I knew. He led me to the car and opened the door for me. As he ran around the vehicle to get to the driver's side, I placed my coffee in the cup holder. My fingers were about to reach for the seatbelt when my entire body froze.

Tiny rhinestones decorated the compartment before me. They came together to form one word: 'Nataliya.'

Kingston came in the car. "We—" He paused as he noticed how drastically my mood had changed. "It's not what it looks like."

I didn't want to be in the car anymore. But I didn't want to call a cab even more. "I'll sit in the back," I said, my voice low.

Kingston scoffed. "This isn't a taxi. Look, I'll just..." He shuffled around until he found a set of keys. He reached over my body, making me get a deep waft of his cologne as he began to scrape at the carefully placed letters.

"Stop that!" I rushed out, my eyes wide. My hands shot to still his hands. "What are you doing? You're going to damage your car."

Kingston looked at me. "Cosmetic damage to a replaceable car is nothing compared to emotional damage to the woman I'm trying to be with."

I faltered.

My hands slipped away from his and laid on my lap. He continued scraping at the letters until most of them were on the floor below my feet.

"We can't be together..." I said in a whisper, though I was unsure if this time the words were meant for him or for myself.

"Why not? We already have our second date planned," Kingston asked while brushing some stray stones off my dress and onto the floor.

My head throbbed. On instinct, my hands reached up to loosen my headscarf, then I remembered I hadn't worn one tonight. "Our conversations feel repetitive at this point."

"Let's change it, then," Kingston said. He sat more upright and stared me dead in the face as he said, "When do you want me to beat your back out again, then put a ring on it?"

The corner of my mouth ticked in amusement. "I see that you get your fast movements from your dad," I teased, but he didn't answer.

His eyes darted to the side, staring through the window behind me. A far-away expression appeared on his face.

Had I hit a nerve? My mouth straightened. A part of me felt bad that I'd ruined his mood. Desperate to steer Kingston's thoughts in another direction, I rushed out the first thing that came to my mind, "Who's the old passenger princess?"

He scowled. "A cheating ex-girlfriend."

I pretended as if I didn't know by frowning. "I'm sorry," I lied, though I really wasn't. After experiencing his dick down my throat and far up my pussy, plus the things he made me feel in this organ beating in my chest, I felt like no one was truly good enough for Kingston Badalo if it wasn't me.

"Don't be," he said, looking back at me. "She led me to you," he said, and I shook my head, already getting used to these types of answers. He smiled, then handed me his phone. "Put in your address."

Kingston and I stood before my apartment door, both looking at each other, unsure what to say. A part of me didn't want the night to end. The other part of me needed to be with my vibrating dildo, just so I could think rationally without a horny haze over my mind.

But I knew whether I had an orgasm tonight, it'd do nothing to erase the things I felt for this man. We'd already crossed all lines, and it was foolish of me to think that I could easily repaint them and move on and pretend that nothing had ever happened.

I fiddled with the cup in my hand. My coffee had gone cold — something that was unheard of with me. And it was all Kingston's fault. He'd spent the entire car ride making me blush like a schoolgirl and asking what I liked to eat so he could carefully curate a charcuterie board for me when he came over for the sip and paint. There hadn't been much room for sipping coffee, but I wasn't complaining.

I cleared my throat. "Well..."

"Can I use your restroom before I go?" Kingston rushed out.

"Uh— Sure—" I went inside the house and closed the door after he entered. I pointed toward the bathroom, thankful that I'd at least closed my bedroom door before I left the house. I didn't know how I'd live with myself if Kingston thought that my room always looked a mess with clothes and shoes everywhere.

While he used the bathroom, I went to the kitchen and tossed the cup. Just as I returned to the living room, I heard the flush of a toilet. Moments later, Kingston reappeared, and we were both standing by the door again.

"Thank you for bringing me home," I said while looking up at him.

"No drive safe and goodnight kiss?" he teased.

"Drive safely."

"And the other part?"

I stared at him. Every feature of this tall, dark, and handsome man committed itself to my memory down to the finest detail — more than enough for me to get myself off later while wishing it could've been him, again, instead.

My eyes lingered on his mouth. I could've kissed those inviting lips. It wouldn't have been the first time. We'd already licked and sucked almost every part of each other's bodies that strangers definitely shouldn't have.

But that was before lines were skewed. Before we even knew that there were lines that could be crossed.

And I couldn't kiss him with that knowledge. Not when I wasn't ready to accept something that was more wrong than it was right.

I tipped and placed my lips on his cheek. Kingston exhaled a quiet, shaky breath. My lips lingered on his skin for longer than was necessary. He turned his head to the side, making my mouth slowly trail across his cheek until it was coming dangerously close to his mouth. My heart went into overdrive.

I called on willpower I didn't know I was capable of at the moment and used it to pull away from him at the very last moment. Our faces remained close to each other, causing my coffee breath and his minty one to mix together while we looked each other in the eyes.

"Goodnight, Kingston," I said, my voice soft.

Knowing the effect he was having on me without even touching me, Kingston smirked. "Goodnight, Miss Grippy."

Chapter Five

WHERE THERE'S A DISAPPOINTMENT, MAKE IT AN OPPORTUNITY

KINGSTON

Blinking fast and hard was doing nothing for my watery vision. I couldn't believe I was about to do this, but the visceral reaction my body had to Nataliya's call a few hours ago made me know that this was something I truly had to do.

Marvyn was right. This co-parenting situation of a dog that we had was insane. I loved Skye with all my heart. Not to say that I was against the idea — because it had always been an 'If it happened, it happened. And if it didn't happen, it didn't happen.' kind of thing for me — but Skye was like a daughter I never had.

I adopted her from a shelter for Nataliya so she had some company when she was home and I wasn't there. Skye was part of a litter that got left at the shelter because the owners were moving out of state and they couldn't foot the costs of caring for their two grown dogs, the puppies, and getting settled in their new home.

Skye grew quickly on Nataliya and me. Every moment was a shared milestone in our lives — Skye going to the vet, her daily walks. Hell, she even had the occasional play date with one of Nataliya's friends' dogs.

But if I wanted a future truly free from the woman who I was starting to hate, then I needed to cut ties with Skye, too.

Skye could sense that something was off with me. I'd been parked outside this house for the past five minutes. Skye was on the dog bed in the passenger seat, and she'd been whining while I stroked her fur and tickled behind her ears.

"I'm going to miss you, girl," I told her and blinked hard again when she whined. I exhaled a heavy breath and looked toward Nataliya's mom's house. When I kicked that lying, conniving cheater out, she had nowhere else to go and went back to live at her mom's place. I grabbed all of Skye's things and her leash, then hopped out of the car. Slowly, I approached the house.

Wanting to spend more time with Skye, who was in no rush by my side.

Wanting to delay meeting the woman who kept peeking through the blinds, ready to open the door and pretend she hadn't heard me clearly when I said I was coming over to drop off Skye.

On the patio, I pressed the doorbell. It rang loudly throughout the house, then I heard shuffling. Skye got excited. She began scratching at the door and barking, a telltale sign that she'd sensed her mother and was happy to see her.

I solemnly smiled at Skye while the locks of the door clicked open in the background. I liked that Skye was happy. She deserved to be. And, despite the fucked up situation Nataliya and I were in, I knew she'd give Skye the world and more until her very last breath.

That thought was the comfort I needed to make this goodbye easier.

Finally, the door opened.

Face-to-face with Nataliya, I felt nothing. I'd spent every waking second since our phone call replaying the moments in my head of how I caught her with her coworker. It made me go through all the fucked up parts of the stages of a fresh breakup, much quicker.

I carried the world on my back just to give it to a woman so she'd never have to worry another day about getting her nails and hair done, getting the love and peace she deserved and getting the orgasms her body craved, but it turned out my efforts weren't good enough for her, then so be it. This was Nataliya's loss, not mine.

"Acheem," Nataliya said, her voice on edge as she broke the silence.

"Here," I said, and transferred Skye's things into her hold. I looked down at Skye, who was now nipping at Nataliya's toes. "Be good," I told Skye and turned around, not waiting to see if she'd acknowledged me. The longer I stayed here, the likelier I'd end up regretting giving up custody of Skye.

"Acheem!" Nataliya yelled toward my back, and I paused, one foot already off the patio, but I didn't look back. "Why're you mad at me when you led me to cheat?"

My jaw tightened. "*Led you*?" I asked through clenched teeth over my shoulder.

"Yes," she answered. "You're always working like a horse. What do you think would've happened when I felt neglected?"

I spun around in a flash. "I worked hard to put that hair on your head, those lashes on your eyes, and that jewelry around your wrists—" I stopped talking. Why was I wasting my breath? "Big up yuself, Nataliya." I walked away while she continued pleading her case to deaf ears. If she knew what I knew, she'd stay the hell away from me after today. If I ever saw Nataliya again, so help me God, I was going to sue her for the lost wages I could've made through picking up extra shifts at Escargot instead of being on that fucking pity cruise.

Marvyn never lied when he told me that in every disappointment, there was an opportunity.

I'd promised my old man that I'd show up to meet his future wife and her daughter, but I'd almost given up on doing so. The journey from Newark to Jacksonville had been hell.

First, Nataliya had made it difficult to leave her mom's place. She'd jumped before my car and said that she wouldn't leave unless we talked things out. I tried several times to drive around her, but the crazy woman kept running around my car with tears streaming down her cheeks and Skye nipping at her toes.

After her mom came home and managed to get Nataliya away from my car with the stern warning to stop embarrassing her in the neighborhood, I finally left. Hoping to still make it in time for my flight, I went straight to the airport.

I didn't make it in time.

No more flights were leaving Newark to Jacksonville until the following night, and I didn't want to just wait around doing nothing. So, I went right back to my car and began the long, thirteen-hour drive to Florida. Thanks to a few energy drinks and Dancehall music blasting from my speakers, I managed to do the drive with no stops outside of the occasional bathroom break or to get gas.

When I finally arrived at the house Marvyn was renting, I went right to the first guest bedroom I saw and was knocked out cold for damn near the whole day. When I finally woke up and saw the time, I knew I was fucked.

I was over an hour late to the dinner, and I knew Marvyn was going to rip me a new one later. Instead of completely flaking, I got dressed and went straight to the restaurant.

Imagine my surprise when I saw Rhyan.

"There really is an opportunity in every disappointment," I said to myself now as I transferred the food items from the grocery bags into the fridge. I'd been on cloud nine since I came home a few moments ago. The feel of Rhyan's soft lips still lingered on my cheek. What I'd give to have her mouth on me like that again.

Hesitant, yet full of so much passion.

She wanted me badly. I'd relentlessly woo her until she learned to stop denying the chemistry between us.

I'd been so determined to be a good son for Marvyn once again, but fuck that. No disrespect to Rhyan's mom, but Marvyn's relationships never lasted long anyway. Unless I bore witness to them signing those papers within three weeks, Rhyan was up for grabs.

And when I grabbed her, I'd hold on forever.

Someone needed to figure something out about how this familial relationship would work, but it for sure wouldn't be me. I already knew what I wanted, and Rhyan would make up her mind soon enough. I'd make sure of it.

My phone rang. My determined grin didn't wash away as I answered it.

Miami, my sister, who was a year younger than me, raised a brow at me. "What are you smiling about?" she asked.

I explained everything to her, but I excluded the details about exactly who Rhyan was. I didn't want to make anyone none-the-wiser about what we had going on until shorty told me out of her own mouth that she wanted us to be together.

"I guess I need to start going on cruises," Miami laughed. "So that's the only reason you're back in Florida? I'm hurt, big brother. I thought you'd come visit me."

"I'll come see you before I go back to Jersey," I promised. Seeing her smile made me feel guilty that I had to ruin her mood with my next words. "Marvyn's trying to get married again..."

Miami's eyes bulged. "W-What?" she asked, aghast, as I nodded. "Tell me everything," she demanded, and I complied while still being mindful of how I mentioned Rhyan's relationship to Robyn. Miami sighed. "Every time I tell you to leave Marvyn alone, it's like I'm wasting my breath."

"How?" I asked, not that I wanted to hear, but I knew she was still going to tell me either way. A part of me was convinced that my sisters just loved hearing themselves talk. Shit.

"He's not good for you. For any of us."

A sigh passed my lips, knowing that Miami was going to say that. "That's different, and you know it."

"Know what?" she argued. "That you don't know who your mom is, but at least we have our moms to fall back on?"

"Exactly that," I said as I began seasoning the meat I was going to cook for tomorrow's dinner.

"You're a grown man now, Acheem. Stop using that excuse. I love you, not Marvyn, and I don't want you around him. You don't know the real him," Miami said in her usual no-nonsense tone.

"He's our *dad*," I said, mimicking her tone. "You and Dallas are always talking in riddles when it comes to Marvyn. If he's so bad, then you need to tell me what he's done to the both of you so that I know how to move around him."

Miami's shoulders drooped. Sadness filled her eyes. "I can't tell you. You love him too much to believe me or Dallas. When you find out, it's going to hurt, but this is something that you have to learn by yourself, on your own time."

I shook my head, annoyed and frustrated by this conversation. I contemplated calling Dallas, my sister who was older than me by two years, but I refrained because it'd make no sense. Marvyn was a great dad; I couldn't imagine him doing anything horrible to them that would cause them and their mothers to hate him so much.

I cocked my head to the side as I heard shuffling from the foyer. "That's probably him..." I said to Miami.

Miami scowled. "Bye, Acheem. Don't let him know that I was talking to you—"

"Hello," Marvyn greeted as he entered the kitchen.

Miami stiffened. She tried and failed to keep the malice out of her eyes as Marvyn stood beside me and looked down on the screen at her.

Tension electrified the room. The noises my hands made as they mixed the meat around to evenly spread the seasonings throughout made some awkwardness permeate the otherwise quiet room.

"Hello, Marvyn," Miami greeted finally.

"I've been trying to get in contact with you for the longest," Marvyn said.

"Lost my phone and had to get a new number," Miami said, which wasn't a complete lie. My sister changed her phone number almost every other year, saying that was how she kept her circle small by getting rid of people who were more like baggage in her life.

"I'm in Florida if you'd like to see me. We'll be here for a while."

"I would, but I'm not in Florida right now," Miami said, and Marvyn just stared at her, causing her to shuffle about as if she feared he was seeing right through her lie. "Well... I'm going to go. Bye, Marvyn. Later, Acheem." She ended the call before either of us could reply.

Marvyn shifted all of his attention to me. "What was she saying?"

"The usual." I shrugged and stuck my hands beneath the tap, washing away all the seasonings.

Marvyn sighed with a shake of his head. He laid a hand on my shoulder and squeezed it once. "Don't believe a word your sisters say. They're just like their moms, always trying to say I'm a bad father and a worse man, but they never shared those sentiments when they tried putting me on child support even when I've been nothing less than an active father in all of your lives."

"I know, Daddy," I said.

Marvyn scowled and pulled his hand away. He put some distance between us. "Wah'm to yu?" he asked, annoyed. "Always spoiling the mood."

I laughed, at ease now that the tension was gone and Marvyn and I were back to our normal selves.

"Explain to me why you were late," he said, his voice stern. "I really needed you to be on time for the good appearances."

I sucked my teeth as I moved to the fridge and stuck the pot of meat in there. "How many kids have you told this one that you have?"

"The truth bent... One," he admitted.

My brow raised. "And the others?"

Marvyn shrugged. "I'll start telling women about them once they start helping me with said women."

I shook my head with a disappointed sigh. "Night, Marvyn," I said as I left the kitchen. It'd been a fucking long day.

Dinner was great. Robyn fell head over heels in love with the garlic parmesan chicken I made. I thought Rhyan loved it too, but that was just me being hopeful. She'd been avoiding eye contact with me and trying not to talk to me more than necessary. It was cute at first, but now as she sat on the sofa across from me while our parents were outside on the balcony talking, I was becoming annoyed with the childish act.

"Rhyan," I called out, and her fingers froze above the phone's screen momentarily before she continued furiously swiping again. Knowing she was probably scrolling through the settings on her phone, I scoffed before standing. I walked over and sat beside her.

She tried scooting away, but there was nowhere to go.

A smirk came on my lips as I took the phone from her hands and placed it behind me on the sofa, out of her reach.

"Kingston," she said sternly, trying to scare me.

Did shorty know how much she was turning me on by doing that?

My grin stretched. "How was dinner, Rhyan?"

"You know."

"I want to hear it from your mouth."

She stared at me for a moment. "Dinner was great, Kingston. Thank you, I enjoyed it."

"You're welcome," I said, smiling.

"The only downside was that you didn't make us any dessert."

"Robyn made the dessert for me already," I said, and Rhyan's eyes widened while her mouth dropped.

"That's inappropriate!"

"How?" I asked, my eyes dropping to her mouth. "I'm ready for my dessert."

A shiver ran through her, and she gulped hard. "I-I—"

"I can eat you on the dining table or on the bathroom counter. You choose. Either way, you're not leaving until I get another taste of you."

She was breathing so hard now that I could vividly hear every inhale and exhale. Her chest rose and fell fast. Her nipples poked against the material of her dress, making me wonder if she'd intentionally chosen not to wear a bra just so she could tease me.

Not that I minded. Rhyan had some small breasts that were the perfect size for me to kiss and suck on. My dick hardened at the thought of having them in my mouth again.

"Kin-gst-on," she forced out. "We can't—"

"Table or counter," I said, my assertive tone plus the look I gave her, leaving no room for an argument.

Rhyan bolted to her feet. I watched as she damn near broke her ankles in those heels while running down the hallway to where the rooms were.

I smirked. Knowing that she was probably in the bathroom in sheer disbelief that we really were about to fuck despite our parents being in the house, I gave her a moment by herself.

When I felt like enough time passed, I adjusted my dick in my pants before I stood. I made my way down the hallway and entered the guest bedroom I claimed for myself. Instantly, I knew she wasn't here. I couldn't smell her strong perfume.

"Ah, fuck," I cursed, realizing she was in Marvyn's room. I'd planned on taking my time with Rhyan, but now I wasn't sure how much time we'd have together. This needed to be quick.

I exited the room and went across the hall to Marvyn's room. As I pushed the door inward, Rhyan's smell enveloped me.

Sweet and soothing jasmine and vanilla.

Her breath hitched as I entered the bathroom while closing the door behind myself. She was already sitting atop the counter, much to my surprise.

"Yet I'm supposed to believe that you don't want this?" I asked as I approached her.

"You didn't give me a choice," Rhyan answered, trying to mask the need in her voice with annoyance.

I chuckled. "You'll always have a choice with me, shorty. You chose to come in here." I put my hands on her thighs, parting her legs so I could stand between them. "You chose to come on this counter." I trailed a hand up her thigh, across her flat abdomen until my hand was wrapped around her neck, squeezing slightly. "You chose to make me fuck you again."

"I..." she trailed off, fumbling for a witty response.

"Stop fighting this," I said.

"I want to," she admitted, nearly throwing me off my game.

My brow raised. "So?"

"So what?" Rhyan asked. "Shut up and kiss me."

My mouth found hers. My thumb caressed the soft skin of her neck as I angled her head to get closer to her mouth. Rhyan's lips parted with ease, making me slip my tongue inside and control the pace in every way I wanted to.

My cock pressed against my pants, aching with need and desperate for a release. My hand on Rhyan's thigh crawled between her legs. I stroked the wet crotch of her panties with two of my fingers, and she trembled against me.

While breaking the kiss, I slipped the panties to the side. My fingers played along her slit as she buried her face into my neck, trying to stifle her moans.

Though I'd love to hear the sweet sounds her witty, stubborn mouth could make, I knew better.

I stopped teasing her clit to slip her panties down her long legs, off her body, and stuff them into her mouth. Taken by surprise, Rhyan's eyes widened. I could tell that she was about to spit it out and curse my ass out, so I slipped my middle finger into her pussy. She melted into my hold, her eyes fluttering closed as they rolled to the back of her head.

"Yeah, baby. Relax for me," I said as my ring finger joined my middle finger. I fingered her pussy hard and fast, curling my fingers upward every so often and making her back arch off the counter. I kissed along her skin, fighting every urge to suck on her skin. I knew her indecisive ass was going to curse me out for fucking her too good again, and I didn't want to hear her mouth more than necessary if I gave her a couple hickies.

I pulled back to watch her. "You gonna come for me?" I asked as I pressed my thumb against her clit.

Moaning quietly, Rhyan nodded. She grabbed my forearm with one of her hands. The other curled around the edge of the counter.

Her eyes flashed open. Rhyan stiffened, and her walls fluttered around my fingers. Watching her lose herself beneath me almost made me come in my pants.

How could one woman be this sexy?

My fingers maintained their pace in her pussy while she rode out her first orgasm. I gradually slowed them down as she came down from her high. I slipped my fingers out of her pussy, took the panties out of her mouth and rested them on the counter.

"Open," I ordered, moving my fingers to her mouth.

Rhyan's mouth loosened without a fuss. She leaned forward and wrapped her lips around my fingers, sucking them into her mouth. She moaned around my fingers while maintaining eye contact with me. My lips parted as she freed my fingers from her mouth and trailed her tongue along the side of my middle finger. Watching her treat my fingers like it was my dick made my need for her grow by the dozen.

"Careful..." I warned, and she smirked. I shook my head at her before dropping to my knees. She threw one of her legs over my shoulders as my head disappeared beneath her dress. I inhaled a deep waft of her pussy, loving her natural feminine scent instead of flowers, fruits, and a pending yeast infection.

I blew on the sides of her thighs, ready to feast on Rhyan's pussy like I hadn't eaten an hour ago, when I remembered our parents would probably start searching for us any moment now.

Instead of taking my time to savor her pussy, I made it quick. I dragged my tongue along her slit over and over, licking away all the traces of her orgasm. When I was done, I pulled back to find her staring at me through darkened eyes. Desire had washed away every trace of doubt, making me solemn that I couldn't treasure this moment as much as I wanted to.

"You're bad for me, Kingston," Rhyan said.

"Maybe," I agreed. "But at least I know how to make you feel good."

She smiled.

I returned the smile as I pulled my wallet out of my pocket for the condom I always kept in there. Then, I dropped my pants and boxers. They puddled around my feet while I slipped the condom on.

I licked my lips as I hooked my arms below Rhyan's knees, tugging her forward to make her lay down. The smell of her pussy still lingered on my top lip, and I pushed my mouth up to smell it.

Rhyan's brows furrowed. "Why're you making that face?"

I chuckled. "No reason," I lied and took my dick into my hand. I tapped my dick atop her pussy, making her shudder, before I lined my tip with her entrance. "Legs around me," I said. "I don't want you running."

"Shut up, Kingston," she laughed while complying. "And make it quick."

"Don't think I have a choice, Miss Grippy," I said as I thrusted inside her. Inch by inch, Rhyan's warmth accepted me. A long, satisfied sigh escaped both of our mouths. I didn't stop until all of me was buried deep inside her. "You good?"

She was looking between us as she nodded. "Yeah."

"Good," I said. "Now do me a favor and put your panties back in your mouth."

After she did, I began to slowly thrust in and out of her. Her heels dug further into my back with every stroke. "Fuck, baby," I groaned, trying not to hasten my pace because I didn't want to come quick even though that was probably for the best.

Rhyan's moans poured into the makeshift gag. One of her hands dragged across my abdomen. I fucking loved the view of my dick going in and out of her pussy. The condom was glistening with her juices. The view made me feral.

My pace quickened.

Rhyan tossed her head back. Her moans were louder now, but still muffled. Her nails dug into my abdomen as she tried pushing me off, but I refused to slow down.

"How could you keep this pussy from me?" I asked. My hand wrapped around her neck. "Don't keep this pussy from me again, Rhyan. I want you and this pussy forever. You hear me?"

She nodded profusely.

I smirked and leaned forward. At an awkward angle, I took her right breast into my mouth. Her pussy gripped around my cock at will while my tongue swirled around her hard nipple. I stopped squeezing her neck and used my hand to grope her other breast.

"Mm. Uh!" Rhyan moaned as I continued to pummel into her.

My orgasm was coming soon. I could feel it building in my gut and tightening my balls. I stopped showing love to Rhyan's breasts and kissed along her cheek. I ripped the panties from her mouth and quickly captured her mouth with mine.

Our kiss was hard.

Messy.

Greedy.

Full of a craving that could never be sated.

As she reached her second orgasm, her arms wrapped around my back. Her walls tightened around my cock, squeezing so tightly I couldn't tell where my body ended and where hers began. Rhyan held me close to her, indicating that she didn't want me to pull out. I groaned, fucking her through my orgasm while my cum flooded the condom. Rhyan's tongue twirled with mine, making me feel a type of ecstasy I hadn't experienced in a long while. My senses became clouded with only Rhyan as its focus. I was hyperaware of everything that made her who she was.

Her smell.

Her taste.

Her touch.

Her.

My breathing was ragged and heavy as my release came to its end. Breathless, I pulled away from Rhyan's mouth. I didn't pull out as I slumped against her. My head rested in the crook of her neck.

"Wow," Rhyan breathed. She dragged her fingers along my back.

I chuckled and pulled back. I gave her lips and nose a quick peck. "Enjoyed dessert?"

She grinned. "Thanks for dinner."

RHYAN

Oh, my God! I couldn't believe I just did that!

I was still in the bathroom, recollecting myself. Kingston had left a short moment ago to check if our parents had missed us, and I knew I was going to hell when I said that I honestly couldn't care less.

If Kingston's knack for cooking, big dick, and cheesy pick-up lines were something I could have forever, I didn't want to pass on the opportunity.

My skin reddened at the thought that I really was about to indulge in this relationship.

Giving myself another once over, I finally decided to leave the restroom. As I opened the bathroom door and was about to exit, I froze in the doorway.

Marvyn had entered the room. He lingered by the doorway too.

My skin flamed all over again. My heart thudded fast in my chest while my eyes widened. “M-Marvyn,” I rushed out. “I’m sorry for being in your room. I was just leaving—”

Marvyn chuckled. “Don’t bite your tongue, Rhyan.”

I nervously chuckled. Not because I had that gut feeling again that something was off with this man and I couldn’t pinpoint what it was, but because the entire room still smelled strongly of hot, passionate sex.

Mortified, I speed walked out of the room.

If Marvyn could smell it, I hoped he wouldn’t mention it to Mom. I wasn’t sure how I’d live with the shame.

And just like that, my post-nut clarity slammed into me like unruly kids robbing me of my car. All the certainty I felt about being with Kingston vanished.

We couldn’t be together.

I was going to hell head way for entertaining the thoughts that we ever could.

Chapter Six

WHERE THERE'S A CABIN, LIGHTS WILL GO OUT DURING A THUNDERSTORM

RHYAN

"Girl, who did you have over here?" Addie shouted from my bathroom a few days later.

My brows furrowed as I racked my brain. "No one," I answered from the kitchen. "You know you and Mom are my only guests," I grumbled as I scrubbed at a pan Addie used.

Like the great best friend she was, she came over, cooked us breakfast, and left me to do all the dishes. I wasn't complaining though. At least I never had to worry about starving once she was around.

Addie really loved to cook. Just like Kingston. I smiled at the memories of that man.

"Well, unless you've started wearing men's watches, whose is this?"

I looked over my shoulder. Addie stood at the entrance to the kitchen, holding a gold wristwatch in her hands.

My mouth dropped. My hands froze in the soapy pan. "No way," I said in sheer disbelief. How hadn't I noticed those?

"Wait..." Addie's eyes flashed between me and the wristwatch, then her eyes brightened. "This is Kingston's?"

"I'm pretty sure," I answered. I quickly dried my hands on a nearby towel and met Addie, who was walking toward me. After taking the wristwatch from her hands, I examined it.

She laughed. "He's trying to mark his territory."

I blushed. "Stop that. We're not together."

"You might as well. What with you two fucking with your parents right in the next room," Addie said, wiggling her eyebrows while I regretted ever telling her anything. "You still haven't told me if you were like, *Oh, step-bro, harder*!"

Laughing from embarrassment, I swatted at her. "You're such a child!"

Addie screamed in laughter. My skin was flaming red now. I prayed the floor would open up and swallow me to save me from this moment, but that never happened. Groaning, I walked out of the kitchen. Kingston's watch was tightly clutched in my palm. Addie followed closely behind me, making kissing sounds that made me wonder if she was thirteen or twenty-three.

I entered my room and placed the piece of jewelry atop my dresser. "You need to leave," I told her as I began making my bed and taking my clothes off the floor to put back in the closet.

Addie sobered up. "Right. I forgot that step-bro is coming over."

"Oh, God," I groaned.

Chuckling, she threw her hands into the air. "I'm leaving. Bye, Rhyan. I love you. Let me know everything!"

"I will," I said grudgingly, both hating and loving that we never kept secrets between each other. Knowing Addie would close up after herself, I went back to cleaning my apartment.

Kingston was coming over today, and I'd be lying if I said that I wasn't even a little nervous to see him again after what we did to each other the last time. There was a lot of work that needed to be done during this sip and paint, so I doubted we'd get the chance to touch on each other's privates, but... I still got a full body wax yesterday after work. Just in case.

By the time I had everything ready and changed out of my pajamas into something more casual, Kingston arrived. When I led him to my bedroom, he paused in the doorway. The knowing smirk dropped from his face.

He saw that I had all the furniture close to the back wall of my room covered. My bed was pushed away from the wall, leaving enough space for a ladder along with all the painting supplies I bought from the store yesterday.

Kingston's eyes dragged to mine. "Rhyan," he said.

I smiled. "Yes, Kingston?"

"You know this isn't what a sip and paint means, right?"

"It is, though. You're going to be painting, and I'm going to be sipping," I said, then gave him the cutest face I could muster. "I thought you wanted to spend time with me."

"Yu know say you a problem," he said, and I smiled at his sexy Jamaican accent even though I didn't understand what he said. Kingston shook his head, then took off his shirt.

I sucked in a breath. My eyes did a greedy take of Kingston's toned, dark skin. His abs were practically begging me to lick them. I salivated at the thought of trailing my tongue along his V-line until his entire dick was down my throat too, leaving behind the taste of his come so I could never forget him.

As his tee lifted above his head, I scooped my mouth up off the floor and pretended I hadn't been gawking at him. Kingston smirked before turning his back to me. He walked over to my wall and got to work.

I sat on a nearby stool, grabbed my glass of wine, and sipped. The view from back here was making my pussy develop its own heartbeat. The way the muscles in Kingston's back flexed made me wonder if that was how they contorted every time we had sex.

I jumped to my feet. Kingston looked around with his brow raised.

"You good?" he asked.

"Yes," I said and forced a smile. No way was I going to tell him that simply watching him made me horny. "You left your watch over here."

"I know."

I scoffed and grabbed his wristwatch off my dresser. "You planned on coming back over here?"

"Something like that," he admitted.

I walked toward him and stopped close. "For your information," I said, and he stopped priming the wall to look at me. "You're the only man in my life."

That made him smirk. "So, is this you accepting that I'm a part of your life?"

"You haven't exactly given me a choice, have you?" I asked, and he chuckled.

Loving the sound, I smiled. "Here," I said, and tucked his watch into his pocket so he wouldn't leave it again. As I pulled back, I got the urge to kiss him, so I leaned forward and placed my mouth on his before I could overthink what we were doing. Kingston kissed me back almost immediately, making me smile into our kiss. When he started putting the brush down, I had to force myself to pull away. "Nah-uh! After you're done with my wall."

He groaned. "You're going to make me paint your wall while I'm horny?"

I looked down, surprised to see a bulge in his pants. "How does one kiss make you hard?"

"Because it's you, Rhyan," Kingston said, making butterflies erupt in my stomach. "Hey, don't hide that pretty smile from me," he said, holding my chin to keep my face in place so that I couldn't look away. My breath came out fast and hard as Kingston stared at me with an intensity I'd never experienced with anyone except him.

"Kingston," I said.

"Baby?"

I smiled. "Let's hurry with the wall before my pussy starts leaking onto the floor."

He roared a loud laugh that made me laugh too. "You're something else, you know?" he asked, and I grinned. "Whoa. What are you doing?" he asked as I reached for a brush.

"I'm going to help you paint," I said.

He shook his head. "Woman, go sit your sexy ass down. As much as I love licking all over your body, I don't think it'll taste great with paint on it."

"We can have shower sex," I suggested.

"This isn't up for debate," he stated firmly, making my pussy moisten even more.

Something about him taking control was so sexy. I loved a manly man!

I put the brush down and returned to the stool. While Kingston painted, we chatted and got to know each other better. We steered the conversation elsewhere every time the topic of our parents came up, to which I was thankful. I was just starting to accept the idea that I liked my future step-brother and wanted more than sex from him, and I wasn't ready to confront the complications that would come with us being together.

"Why sky blue?" Kingston asked, halfway through the second layer of paint on my backdrop.

"It reminds me of the views from the cruise," I answered. Reminiscing made me crave another cruise. Maybe to a different Caribbean island this time. Outside of visiting every state in America — one of the perks that came with moving around a lot as I grew up in a military family — I didn't travel much. I wasn't getting any younger, and the trip to Jamaica made me truly face the fact that there was a whole other world out there for me to get a first-hand experience of.

Kingston smiled. As he opened his mouth to say something, the doorbell cut him off. My brows furrowed. I wasn't expecting anyone. Curious, I stood, then froze.

The ringing still hadn't stopped.

"Mom," I whispered, my life flashing before my eyes. I looked at Kingston, whose carefree experience made me wonder if I was overreacting by being on the verge of a panic attack. "Hide!" I hissed at him and rushed over before he could reply. I snatched the brush from his hand and dropped it on the plastic on the floor while pushing Kingston toward my tiny closet.

The incessant ringing was my sole focus; I didn't have time to lust over how Kingston's back felt beneath my fingertips. Kingston looked so out of place, smushed into my closet. I frowned at him. "Sorry."

"It's fine. I love cramped spaces," he said sarcastically, and I rolled my eyes at him before running out of the room.

The doorbell went quiet as I opened the door.

"Bestie!" Mom greeted and threw her arms around me.

My arms wrapped around her. "Hi, Mom," I said, hoping she couldn't somehow feel how hard my heart was beating or hear the nervousness in my voice.

"What are your plans for today?" she asked as she broke the hug and entered the house. "And why does it smell like paint?" she asked, and glanced toward my bedroom.

My eyes widened as I spotted Kingston's shirt on my bed, and the two half-empty glasses of our drinks. I bolted toward the door and slammed it shut. Mom gave me a puzzled glance.

"Are you okay?" she asked.

I nodded. "Yes, Mom. I-I just—" I cleared my throat. "My room's a mess."

"That's nothing new for you, Rhyan."

I gasped. Could Mom's mouth be any louder? I really hoped Kingston hadn't heard that. I forced a smile. "It's just really bad because I'm repainting. I wanted a change of scenery."

"So you won't be able to go out on a girls' date with me?" she asked with a frown.

"No, Mom," I replied. Today was my day off, and no way would I spend the day listening to her talk about her man and ignore all my pleas to stop showing off her body for everyone to see.

"That's fine. We can just stay in, and I'll help you paint," she said, and walked forward.

"No!" I rushed out, splaying both my arms on either side of me to bar the room.

Mom gasped. Then, she frowned. "You don't have to yell at me, Rhyan. I've never yelled at you. You c-could've just told m-me no."

Guilt slapped me across the face as I listened to Mom's voice break. "Mom, I'm sorry," I said and pried myself away from the door. I hugged her as she sobbed against my body. Sometimes, Mom carried herself so well that I easily forgot how sensitive she got whenever it came to me. I rested my chin atop her head while I patted her back. "I didn't mean it like that. We can go out together. I'm sorry."

"I don't understand why you hate me this much, Rhyan."

I gasped. I pulled her away from me and looked into her teary eyes. My guilt was near stifling now. Tears formed in my own eyes. Fuck. I was such a shit daughter.

"Mom, I don't hate you. I love you with my entire heart. I didn't mean to yell at you. Really. I just don't want help."

"Okay, Rhyan..." she said and dried her face. "I love you, too."

I smiled. "I know, Mom. I'll go get ready, then we can go, okay?" I asked, and she nodded.

Mom took another sip from the complimentary cocktail before placing the glass on the table beside her. She looked over at me, already watching her because I was overly invested in our conversation after I brought tears to her eyes earlier. "I promised to continue giving you the world after Jayden died," she said. "You worked hard to get your Psychology degree and are doing a job that you love. My life's goal is complete, now I can go live my life for me."

I sighed. Wanting to choose my words carefully, I looked away. I focused on the nail tech sitting on the stool before me. The massage chair vibrated my back and ass, trying to relax me, but it was failing miserably. Aside from this conversation that I was having with Mom, I was on edge from knowing that I'd left Kingston in my apartment to finish painting.

I really hoped he wasn't a thief.

"I'm just worried about you, Mom," I confessed.

"About what?"

I looked back at her. "I want you to be happy, but that doesn't mean that I'm not allowed to worry about you. This is the first time I'm seeing you take someone this seriously after Dad. Yes, Marvyn seems like a nice guy, but I just wish you weren't moving this fast with him. You're getting married. You've told him all about Dad's benefits and money. You have him moving from Jersey to come live with you. I just..." I sighed. "I just don't want you to make a mistake, Mom."

A motherly smile came on her face. She reached an arm toward me, and I leaned closer to her. She palmed my face sweetly, and I leaned into her touch. "I appreciate you, Rhyan. I love the way you care for me, and I, you. But, trust me, baby, I know what I'm doing. Your father loved me so much that I know how I should be loved. If a day ever comes when Marvyn does something that no man who says they love me would do, then I'd break off the relationship immediately."

Nodding, I exhaled a breath of relief. "Okay, Mom."

Her smile never faltered as she moved her hand from my face. She reached for her drink again. As she took a sip, her phone rang. She answered it on speaker, letting me know it was Marvyn.

While listening to their conversation, I pretended to be completely invested in watching the man do my pedi.

"Where are you, baby?" Marvyn asked Mom.

"Out with Rhyan," she said before pushing her phone in my face. After I waved at the man, who waved back, Mom moved the phone.

"I can drop by to pay for both of your nails," Marvyn offered.

I hated that I found that thoughtful and sweet. Ugh. Maybe he really wasn't a bad man, and that was why I couldn't shake this foreboding feeling — I kept searching for reasons to paint him differently.

Fine. After today, I'd no longer search for reasons to hate Marvyn or hope Mom would break up with him. With him getting divorced four times and Mom losing her childhood love, they both deserved to be happy.

But... where would that leave me and Kingston?

We needed to figure this out quickly.

"I have an idea," Marvyn was saying now. "Hey, Rhyan?"

I cleared my throat and accepted the phone from Mom. "Yes?"

"You and Acheem could go down to the cabin together to get stuff ready," he suggested, and I stiffened. "I think that'd be better than Robyn and I getting our own honeymoon cabin together," he laughed, and I forced one.

Floor, swallow me now.

Did Marvyn have any idea what he just said? How could he expect me to spend an entire weekend in another town all alone with his son? There'd be no one to stop me from making Kingston leave an imprint of his dick in my throat.

"Oh, that'd be great!" Mom said, beaming. "What do you think, Rhyan?"

"I think it'd be just perfect," I said, and Mom cheered as I handed the phone back to her.

For the past week, I'd been on edge. Today was the day that I'd be driving out of Jacksonville to get the cabin ready for Mom's and Marvyn's wedding next week. Why was time moving so fast? It was hard to believe that they had already knew each other for a month.

Being this nervous wasn't good for me. It brought back memories of me being in college, on edge about exams that I had to take, and it led to me developing a bad habit.

Weed.

I was sitting in the car in front of the house at the address a friend gave me. I hadn't done weed since I graduated. Caffeine and alcohol had become my favorite poisons, but they wouldn't be strong enough to quell my nerves. Why was I even so nervous, anyway? It wouldn't be the first time Kingston and I spent hours locked in one place, all alone.

I exhaled a heavy breath. "Rhyan, relax," I said in an effort to calm myself before I exited the car. Dark clouds hovered in the sky while I walked toward the wooden fence at the side of the one-storey house. I pressed the fob in my hand several times. The car *beeped* in response.

Mom had insisted that I drive her car for the journey. She said that she was okay with me being stubborn in Jacksonville about not being ready to buy a car and refusing all her offers to buy me one, but she wouldn't accept my stubborn answer when it involved me being far out of her reach.

At the gate, I greeted a short, dark skinned man. He spoke in code, so I told him the name of my friend for him to drop the act. He relaxed enough to hand me the baggie through the fence and accept the money from my hands. After I thanked him, I turned, about to walk back to the car, when a female voice stopped me.

"Wow, Miss Fagan," came the voice again.

I froze.

Of all the things that could happen to me today, why did it have to be this? Even if the sky opened up and released its heavy shower of an incoming thunderstorm onto me, it wouldn't have even dented this load that was my shame.

Despite being caught red-handed, I tucked the baggie into the pocket of my jean jacket before turning around. Zayria smiled at me through the wooden fence.

"Zayria," I said, knowing it made no sense to pretend I didn't know who she was. "Please keep this between us."

As Zayria chuckled, the dark-skinned man raised a brow as he looked between us. "Jit, you know her?"

"She's a counselor at school," Zayria said, nodding at the man before giving me her full attention. "Miss Fagan, why would I tell anyone? You're one of the coolest counselors at school, and you have a full sleeve tattoo. I'm not surprised that you smoke."

I opened my mouth to argue her damn-near labelling me as an example of a stereotype, then I closed it. Not only was this situation inappropriate, but I didn't owe Zayria an explanation. I looked at the man, who I now realized must've been a family member of Zayria, if their slight resemblance was anything to go by. "Zayria is a talented student and great athlete. You should look into getting her into a local softball team."

The man nodded. "I will," he promised, and Zayria smiled.

I smiled at them before speed walking away. The sky was darker now, the occasional streak of lightning flashing across the sky while thunder rumbled. As I sat behind the wheel, I sent a quick prayer to God, telling him that I was just joking about the sky opening up and washing me away.

I had a long journey ahead of me with an even longer dick to sit on all weekend, and I didn't want to be delayed.

Sitting before the cabin made me realize this place truly earned its name. The Schadey Cabins were on the outskirts of a small town called Hopewellston. Visibility was extremely limited by fog and how heavily the rain was pouring now, but if I squinted just enough, I could make out the silhouettes of tall trees surrounding the dark wood cabin.

I brought my head down, resting it atop the steering. Large raindrops beating against the car, splattering all over it, made me know this thunderstorm didn't plan to pass over this side of Florida anytime soon.

Maybe it was a bad idea for me to haste to be in a town that was located in the middle of nowhere.

"I'll just wait to see," I told myself, trying to be optimistic despite shivering from the cold.

Ten more minutes passed.

"Nevermind," I said and grabbed my bag off the passenger seat. There was a few stuff in the trunk, but I could just grab them tomorrow. I held my bag close to my chest before hopping out of the car. Frigid rain seeped into my headscarf and clothes as I slammed the door closed and bolted toward the patio.

I shivered as I pressed the fob to the car and fumbled around in my bag for the cabin key. After I found it, I entered the cabin. I gasped at Kingston, who was before a fireplace, stoking at low embers.

"Kingston," I said, but he didn't hear me. Realizing how loud the rain was, I yelled his name.

He startled before looking back at me. His expression morphed into shock before his face relaxed as he smiled. "Rhyan," he said and stood.

"Why're you here? I thought you were coming tomorrow," I said and finally closed the door. Despite the cold air not blowing into the spacious room, it was still freezing cold. I flickered the nearby light switch, then frowned.

"The power went out a few minutes ago," Kingston said.

"Of course," I said, not surprised at the shit luck I had all day.

"The generator didn't kick in, so I went outside to check on it, but it made no sense because I could barely see anything. I just came back in and was trying to get the fire started."

"Thank you," I said, smiling despite trembling. "Why—"

"How about you get out those wet clothes first?" Kingston asked. "I don't want you getting sick."

I nodded without a fuss. While he went back to the fireplace, I went to a room and changed out of my soaked clothes for some pajamas. I texted Mom to let her know I arrived safely, but the message didn't go through. I hoped the cell service would come back soon. Mom would be worried sick about me, and I didn't want her to be.

When I returned to the living room, Kingston had the fire going. "Thanks," I said as I sat on the ground at a safe distance from it.

"I thought you were coming tomorrow," he said, making me think of our earlier conversation because I also thought the same.

"Miscommunication, I guess." I wrapped my arms around my body.

Kingston stopped towering over me to walk to a nearby sofa. He grabbed the blanket off it, then sat beside me. "You'll be warmer if I hold you," he said, wrapping the blanket around our bodies. He wrapped one of his arms around my shoulder.

"Thank you," I said, smiling as I laid my head on his shoulder. The lighting still wasn't the best, but I could admire the beauty of the place. "Have you been here before?"

Kingston nodded. "I've done catering here before. It looks better in the sunlight."

Miserable from the cold and the generator teasing us, I scoffed. "I wouldn't waste a penny on this place."

Kingston laughed. "Don't be like that. The Schadey Cabins are great. When this storm passes and everything's up and running, you'll love it, I promise."

I leaned off his shoulder to look at him. "So, what do you want to do until then?"

A mischievous glint came in his eyes. "I brought a bottle of alcohol to keep my company until tomorrow."

"I brought weed to keep mine."

We broke away from each other to gather our poisons before returning to the floor. Now sitting before each other with our own blankets draped over our shoulders, Kingston and I rode out the thunderstorm together. On the floor between us, there was a bottle of dark liquor, a bag of chips, and a bag of weed. We shared the bottle while passing the blunt back and forth.

Kingston chuckled while I moved the bottle from my mouth with a grimace. "Brings back memories?"

"Whatever," I laughed and handed the bottle back to him. I startled as a loud clap of thunder came. "How many inches of rain are we going to get? This is outrageous," I grumbled as I reached for my phone to check.

Still no service.

"It depends," Kingston answered as he moved the blunt to his lips.

Blindly placing my phone to the side on the floor, my brows furrowed at Kingston. "Depends?" I asked, confused.

He took a long drag from the blunt. He held the smoke, his eyes narrowing slightly on me. My clit throbbed at the way he looked at me. So erotic. So needy. So desperate for every part of me. He blew the smoke towards me, and I inhaled it like an addict.

"On how many inches you can take."

I gasped. "Kingston!"

Grinning, he placed the blunt on the plate we found in the kitchen and were using as a makeshift tray. He curled a finger at me. I crawled over the bag of chips and weed until I was before him.

Kingston's hand locked around my neck. "I told you what you saying my name does to me."

A giggle escaped me. "What? This?" I asked and palmed his dick in his sweats. He sucked in a breath as I rubbed him. "I know, and I don't care."

"Rhyan," he said, his voice low in a warning.

I giggled again. Then, I reached for the bottle and turned it to my head while his hand still loosely held around my neck. I put the bottle back onto the floor, then took Kingston's face into my hand. As I moved closer to his face, he realized what I intended to do, so he opened his mouth.

I spat the alcohol into his mouth. He swallowed like such a good boy for me. My pussy throbbed hard as he held my gaze, forbidden desire pooling in his eyes. I reached forward and stuck my tongue into his mouth, getting every taste of alcohol and his spit.

Kingston moaned. His hand moved from my neck to tighten in the strands of my hair. His other hand wrapped around my waist, keeping me in position atop his cock. I rolled my hips as we kissed hard.

His hand moved from my waist, caressing the small of my back for a moment before it reached for the hem of my shirt. I broke from the kiss, panting hard as Kingston pulled my top off my body.

"No bra," he said.

"You expected different?"

Kingston smirked. "No," he answered, then captured one of my nipples with his mouth.

"Mm," I moaned, tossing my head back and pushing my chest out. I held the back of his head, wanting him to take all of my little breasts into his mouth.

Kingston's other hand palmed my free breast. His tongue swirled around my nipple with fervor. Kingston knew my body like magic because somehow he managed to make me feel those sensations all throughout my body.

"Oh," I drawled, dragging my teeth across my bottom lip as he continued to show love to my titties. "Kingston, I want you."

His mouth released my breast. He kissed along my chest, asking between each contact his mouth met with my skin, "Where do you want me, Rhyan? Talk to me."

"I want to suck your dick. I miss doing it," I said earnestly.

He chuckled, then pulled back. He rested his hands on either side of his body. "Well, don't let me stop you."

I licked my lips and came off his lap. He helped me take his sweats and boxers off. His dick saluted me, already dripping pre-cum from its tip.

I took his dick into my hand. It throbbed. "You missed me, didn't you?"

"Badly," Kingston answered, his voice strained.

I rubbed my thumb across his tip, playing in the pre-cum. "All of this is for me?"

Kingston smirked. "I told you it depends on how much of it you can take."

I glared at him. "All of it. Stop playing with me," I said, then took him into my mouth. As his dick hit the back of my throat, Kingston hissed and tossed his head back. My eyes glistened as I watched him lose himself above me.

I moaned and gagged around his cock as I sucked him. Kingston's hands were balled into fists by his side. Oh, how I missed this dick.

How I missed turning him out.

His dick tasted just right on my tongue. His balls fit well into my mouth.

I licked and sucked everywhere on him. Desperate for all of him, unable to ever get enough.

"Fuck, Rhyan," Kingston moaned.

Knowing he was close, I sucked him faster. Not only did I want him to flood my mouth with his cum, but because I also had a point to prove. I wanted him to know that I could please him just as good as he pleased me. I wanted all of our moments together to be embedded in his brain until he didn't care if our relationship was wrong, right, or everything in between.

"Shit," he hissed as I made his dick stay in my throat for a few seconds so he could savor the warmth. He dragged his gaze from the ceiling and looked down at me. "Don't make me come."

My brows furrowed as I pulled back just enough so I could breathe.

"I want that pussy dripping all over my face while you suck me," he said, and my heart skipped a beat. Kingston had a way of making even the naughtiest things sound romantic. As I freed his dick from my mouth and wiped the spit away that had gathered beneath my chin, Kingston laid back. "Come, shorty. Take a seat."

I kicked off my pants and panties before I sat on his face. As I leaned over to take his cock into my hands again, I felt Kingston inhale a deep waft of my pussy before his tongue dragged along my slit, licking away all the wetness that had gathered there.

I trembled.

Kingston smirked into my pussy.

His smugness refueled my determination to make him come. I took him into my hands, then locked my mouth around his tip. I kissed and sucked on the soft head while he swirled his tongue around my clit.

Noises escaped our full mouths — so loud that the heavy rain barely drowned us out.

Every part of my body was on fire as Kingston ate my pussy like a starving man.

I couldn't focus on sucking his dick. My hold around his shaft loosened. I moaned unabashedly while two of his fingers continued to thrust in and out of my hole while his tongue lapped at me.

"Kingston!" I screamed as my orgasm took full control of me. My eyes snapped shut tight, and my entire body stiffened. This sweet feeling spread from my clit and traveled everywhere within me.

My legs.

My mind.

My heart.

I wasn't sure if I would ever come down from this high if Kingston's dick didn't jerk in my hand before something warm splattered against my cheek. My eyes snapped open to see Kingston coming everywhere.

Wow.

Did I have that much of an effect on him for him to come from eating my pussy and hearing me moan his name aloud?

Despite not having caught my breath, I locked my mouth back around Kingston's cock, then I sucked him dry.

After he flooded my mouth, I toppled off him. I laid next to him on the floor, hoping to catch my breath, but Kingston shuffled around.

His arms hooked around my back, pulling me up off the floor and making me straddle him. His fingers brushed over the mole on my lower back. "There you are."

I chuckled and swatted his hand away. "Stop."

Kingston laughed. His hand reached between us, and I was sinking onto his cock before I could catch my breath.

My back arched as my arms tightened around his broad shoulders. "Kingston…" I drawled.

"Yes, baby?" he said in between kissing my chest.

I moaned incoherent words while I rode him. As my eyes fluttered closed, I caught a glimpse of the flickering flame from the fireplace, casting shadows against the opposite wall.

I looked so good taking Kingston's dick.

With my titty in his mouth. Nails clawing at his back. And his fingers groping my ass.

"I'm close," I announced, my walls tightening around him as he thrusted up into me harder. My eyes were squeezing together much tighter now as I accepted the ferocious strokes.

"Tell me this pussy is mine," Kingston said.

"It's yours, baby," I answered. "Yours and no one else's."

Kingston chuckled. Dark and deep. He smirked against my skin as he kissed up my chest. His mouth found mine, and we kissed sloppily.

"Mm," I moaned into his mouth. My hands rubbed along his sweaty back while the sweet sounds of our slapping skin filled the room. As Kingston's tongue tangled with mine, I lost control of myself.

My orgasm captured me whole.

My lips tingled oh so sweetly as Kingston kissed and fucked me through this moment of bliss. My pussy clenched around his cock, never intending to let go. I wasn't worried about him coming in me. All his kids had already traveled down my throat, I was sure he couldn't go again—

Kingston groaned. I stiffened atop him as warmth flooded my insides. My eyes flew open as I broke the kiss. "Kingston!" I exclaimed, unable to truly admire how sexy he looked as he came, because I was too busy trying to hop off him.

His hands swooped around my waist. He held me in place. Forced me to accept all of him until he came down from his high. "I'll get you a pill in the morning," he panted, then flashed me a lazy grin. "But I wouldn't mind having an 'R' named baby girl."

I wasn't sure if I was supposed to cry or laugh. Undecided, I sagged against him with my head resting on his shoulder and my hands loosely thrown around his waist while his dick remained inside my still throbbing pussy. Kingston stroked his hand along my back in small, soothing circles. Our chests rose and fell in unison. I couldn't believe what he'd just said, or that Kingston had just fucked me so good, I was seriously contemplating telling him not to get me a pill tomorrow.

Chapter Seven

Where There's a Window, Be a Peeping Tom

Kingston

Waking up with Rhyan tucked beneath my arms was something I could get used to. I would've preferred if we were in her newly painted room or my high-rise apartment so that I could better appreciate this view and moment, but I wasn't complaining.

The thunderstorm had passed, and sunlight was streaming through the windows. My arm was slightly cramped from having Rhyan's big ass head on it all night, but I wasn't complaining. I pulled her closer, inhaling a deep waft of her smell and smiling as she stirred in my hold.

Rhyan slept like a log. During the night, I woke up a few times from how loud the thunder was, but Rhyan had yet to show a sign of disturbance.

Her back was pressed against my front, so I couldn't see her face, but I could just imagine how peaceful she looked. With my morning wood pressing hard against her back, I contemplated sticking just the tip inside her pussy, feeling her warmth until she woke up making that beautiful, captivating face she made whenever she was coming, but I decided against it. Rhyan and I hadn't discussed our kinks outside of the basics that got us off, so I wasn't sure how she felt about somnophilia.

She'd barely just started to accept that she was mine regardless of our parents being in a relationship, and I didn't want her to wake up screaming bloody murder while I was fucking her.

As she stirred in my arms again, I placed a soft kiss atop her bonnet before carefully getting out of bed. I knew the owner of the Schadey Cabins kept the place in good condition, so I needed to check what was up with the generator.

I stretched at the side of the bed before making my way to the ensuite bathroom. The electricity was back, so that was good. After I got ready for the day, I went outside. I inspected the generator, but there was nothing wrong with it.

"Weird," I said before heading back inside. Inside a storage closet, I found a fishing rod and headed to the nearby lake. People weren't supposed to fish in this lake without a license, but no one was around to see me. I doubted two fish would hurt the population.

After I caught the fish, I went back to the cabin and began making breakfast for Rhyan and I. It'd been a while since I ate fried fish and fried dumplings. I hoped Rhyan liked it.

As I was frying the last dumplings, tiny arms wrapped around my waist. Rhyan kissed my back, making me smile. "Good morning, handsome," Rhyan said.

I looked over my shoulder at her. "Finally up?"

Rhyan nodded against my skin as she pulled back. "I slept great."

I plated the dumplings, turned off the stove, and then faced her. "My arm knows all about it."

She laughed. "I would say sorry, but I'm not." Her eyes glanced at the plate as I offered it to her. "Thank you."

"You're welcome," I said as we walked toward the table. "There's no coffee here, so—"

"I have some in my car. I'll go get it," she said and stood from the chair.

I laughed as she bolted out of the house. I'd never met such a passionate coffee lover until Rhyan. It was a miracle her teeth weren't stained brown from the substance.

She returned a moment later and made her morning fuel. She offered to make me a cup, but I declined and opted for drinking a bottle of water. She joined me at the table again, and we mostly ate in silence until we were down to the last bits of our food.

"So..." Rhyan said.

"Ready to talk?" I asked.

Nodding, Rhyan pushed her empty plate away from her. She propped up a leg in the chair and rested her chin atop her knee. "How will we tell our parents about us?"

"We'll just tell them."

Rhyan scoffed. "Mom will have a heart attack if I just tell her that her fiancé's son is going to be my boyfriend."

"Going to be?" I asked and mocked her scoff. "Shorty, after last night, there's no confusion about where we stand," I said, and her skin reddened. Knowing that she was thinking of us fucking in every corner of this house, only ever pausing for a water break, until we were both too tired and had no choice but to call it a night, I smirked. "Marvyn doesn't concern himself with my relationships. He won't care."

"Mom doesn't either, but it won't be so simple this time. I don't think she'd be able to look at me the same," Rhyan said. "Plus, what would people say?"

"Fuck people."

"Kingston."

"Fine," I said, then went quiet to think of a rational solution. "Marvyn told me that he and Robyn are planning to move in together. Do you know when Robyn's leaving Florida?"

Rhyan's brows furrowed. "Mom would never leave Florida. She told me Marvyn's moving in with her."

"Weird..." I said. "Since I was a kid, Marvyn hasn't stayed in one place for too long."

"Hmm... Then, I'm not sure. Maybe they're still deciding."

I shrugged. "Well, if she doesn't leave Florida, you could always come back to Jersey with me. No one would ever have to know about our parents' relationship."

She held up a hand. "Slow down, Kingston. When did *I* say that I want to leave Florida, or even live with you? We've known each other for a month."

"And I know we want each other for the rest of our lives, so what's the difference?" I asked, and she reddened again. I shook my head. "You love complaining just to complain, don't you?"

"No," she said. "I just like when you get all manly and take charge."

"So we'll live in Jersey if our parents live here, okay?" I said, and she gave me a delayed nod. "Good. And stop worrying your pretty head about whether or not they'll accept our relationship. We aren't related by blood, and we're two grown adults. The whole step siblings thing doesn't matter."

With a small smile on her face, Rhyan nodded. She opened her mouth to reply, then my phone rang. Intending to ignore the call, I didn't look at the caller ID. The ringing captured Rhyan's attention. As the smile faded from her face, I looked down at the phone's screen.

Shit.

Nataliya.

I declined the call, and my head snapped up to look at Rhyan. "Me and her are over. You have nothing to worry about. It's not what it looks like," I rushed out.

Rhyan wasn't moved as my phone rang again.

I sighed and stood. "I'll be back," I said and went outside through the back door. "What?" I growled into the phone after I answered.

"Acheem," Nataliya said. "Skye hurt her paw, and I was wondering if you could come pick us up so I could bring her to get it checked at the vet?"

Aggravated, I pinched the space between my brows. "Nataliya, I've never called a woman a bitch before. Please don't let today be that day. We are over. I'm going to block you now. Have a nice life with Greg." I ended the call and blocked her number. I tucked my phone into my pocket before going back into the cabin. My stomach sank when I didn't see Rhyan where I'd left her. "Rhyan?" I called out, but got no response.

Sighing, I searched the cabin. I found her out by her car, unloading some cleaning supplies and decorations out of her trunk. "Let me get that for you," I said while approaching her.

"No thanks," Rhyan gritted out.

I blocked her path. "Baby," I said. "I thought I'd blocked her. I'm sorry."

"No, it's fine," Rhyan said. "It doesn't matter if you do or don't have anything going on with her. I was just being silly. We're going to be *family*. Blood or not, we can't be together."

My jaw clenched as she side-stepped me. Rhyan's hot-and-cold attitude was bugging the fuck out of me. She climbed the stairs and disappeared into the cabin. How could one phone call bring us back to square one after we'd made such good progress a few moments ago?

I sighed.

Maybe Rhyan was right. We shouldn't be together. Not because we were going to be a family, but because she still had some growing up to do.

RHYAN

Kingston and I had been avoiding each other for the past few hours. He'd been outside cutting enough wood for our parents so that Marvyn wouldn't have to hassle himself with doing it when they arrived for their one-week stay. I'd been inside, cleaning and putting air fresheners everywhere. The house smelled strongly of the fake roses I used to decorate a trail to the bedroom, where I used towels to make kissing swans atop the bed.

I couldn't believe that I was getting Mom ready to give her away to another man, but that was just life.

The unexpected should always be expected.

But I hadn't expected to have such an angry reaction to seeing Kingston's ex calling his phone. I knew they were over, but a hot flash of jealousy had crossed me at seeing her name on his phone screen. Sure, he'd seemed more annoyed by the call than I'd been, and he'd apologized like the gentleman he was, but my pride refused to leave and allow me to apologize to him.

A heavy sigh passed my lips. I left the bedroom and moved to a window by the kitchen. From here, I could peek at Kingston. He had his back turned to me while he raised the axe in the air, then brought it down quick and hard against a piece of wood, chopping it into two pieces. Sweat rolled down his body, making his dark skin glisten beneath the sunlight. Watching the muscles in his back and strong arms flex made me feel things I didn't have the right to feel at the moment.

Yet... I couldn't stop myself from cupping my pussy. Rubbing myself through my shorts. Imagining it was Kingston playing with me like this.

I needed him badly. I should apologize so we could have hot and angry makeup sex, then lay together afterwards and discuss how we were going to maneuver our lives in New Jersey.

My phone rang. Kingston froze while I did the same.

"Shit," I cursed, ducking below the window before he could turn his head and see me. My fingers fumbled over each other as I reached for my phone in my pocket. Phone in hand, I quickly answered. "Mom," I answered while crawling on all fours out of the kitchen, heading toward the living room.

"Baby," Mom greeted, breathing a sigh of relief.

I smacked my forehead with my hand as I reached the living room and stood. "I'm so sorry for not calling yesterday," I apologized while sitting on the sofa. "Cell service went out last night, and I'd been so busy all morning."

"I figured because I just got your texts. But I still wanted to hear your voice, so I knew you were actually safe," she said. "If I'd known that the thunderstorm would've started earlier than predicted, I would've made you carpool with Acheem today. Is he there yet?"

"Yes, since—" I paused, realizing it wouldn't have made a difference whether or not I told her that me and Kingston had been cooped up together since last night. "He's here."

"Good," Mom said, and I imagined her beautiful smile. "Depending on what time you get done there, don't leave tonight. You can drive back to Jacksonville tomorrow."

"I'd prefer to leave tonight. I didn't know that Hopewellston was in the middle of nowhere," I joked, and she laughed.

"It's a lovely small town. You should go check it out before you come home."

"Hmm. I'll think about it," I said, noticing a cum stain on the couch. I made a mental note to clean it.

"Well, you'll have no choice because I called to tell you what kinds of foods Marvyn and I want you to stock the fridge with."

"My title's changed from daughter to servant?" I asked, and she laughed. I smiled at the sound. When Mom was happy, it made me happy times ten. I opened the notes app on my phone and made a list of every item she said she wanted. After she made me promise to let her know if I was coming back tonight or tomorrow morning so I could get enough rest for work the following day, we kissed each other through the phone before ending the call. My eyes roamed over the list as I stood from the sofa and made my way back to the kitchen, right as Kingston entered.

We stiffened.

Stared at each other.

Never said a word.

He broke the stare first. Then, he dragged a rag across his face, wiping away the sweat as he began walking out of the kitchen.

"Kingston," I called out, and he stopped walking but didn't turn around. A frown came on my face while my heart sank. Unintentionally placing a wedge between us made me miss his smiles and flirtatious jokes. "I'm going into town. Do you want to come with me?" I asked and held my breath while hoping he'd accept the olive branch.

"Sure," he said after a moment, loosening the tension from my shoulders. "Let me go have a shower first."

"Okay," I said, smiling at his back as he walked further into the room. "Yes!" I quietly cheered and pumped my arm when he was out of reach. I wouldn't tell him I was sorry, but so long as he didn't do anything else to piss me off, I'd be sure to make it up to him.

Silently, Kingston pushed the shopping cart in a convenience store called Sylvia's. I strolled beside him, grabbing items off the shelves and putting them in the cart.

The morning-after pill was the first thing I'd grabbed when we got here.

"This is kind of nice," I said suddenly as we went onto another aisle.

"What?" he asked, his voice gruff.

"This. Us. Just doing what normal couples do without thinking about other people."

Kingston looked at me for the first time since we left the cabin. He stopped pushing the cart and faced me, making me turn to face him, too. "See, this could all be so simple if you give us an actual chance instead of changing your mind every other minute," he said, a trace of anger in his tone.

I sighed. "And I wish you'd stop making it seem so simple when you know it isn't. Yes, I want you, Kingston, but not if it's at the cost of robbing Mom of the chance of being in another happy relationship."

"This isn't about Robyn. It's about you, Rhyan—" He paused. "Wait, you never told me your middle name."

"Because I don't have one."

"Hm. Well, it's about *you*, Rhyan Fagan. *Me. Us.* What do you want?"

"You know."

He shook his head. "Say the words, Rhyan."

"After I've spoken to Mom," I said.

Kingston's lips parted slightly. He stared at me with such disbelief, it was crippling. He snapped his mouth shut while shaking his head, then walked away. "What's next on the list?" he grumbled from up ahead, sounding over this shopping trip.

Sighing, I took long strides to catch up with him. "Why can't this just be an extended one-night stand until I work up the courage to speak to her?"

Kingston came to another sudden halt. I almost bumped into his back. He snapped around, staring down at me with a glare.

"Don't say those words to me," he said through clenched teeth. "I want us to be more. I'm not going to keep fucking you good while you keep me a secret."

"A one life stand, then?" I suggested.

Kingston chuckled, though not from amusement. "Am I a joke to you, Rhyan?"

I shook my head. "Of course not."

"Then grow up," he said, spinning around and walking to the cashier despite us not being done shopping.

Stupefied, my mouth dropped. I wasn't sure why Kingston hadn't realized that I was just trying to joke around to get back on his good side until I returned to Jacksonville and confessed to Mom about our relationship, but whatever.

I wasn't childish.

He was the one who needed to grow up. He was being way too uptight for my liking. It was so unlike him, and I hated it.

If leaving my home in Florida to live in New Jersey would consist of a life as strict as this, then maybe my decision not to chase Kingston was for the best.

Whatever.

I wasn't hurt.

I didn't care.

I never wanted a one life stand with him anyway.

Chapter Eight

WHERE THERE'S A MEMORY LANE, WALK AWAY FROM IT

KINGSTON

I got back to Jacksonville a few hours ago, and I'd been at Marvyn's rental since then. I was cooking dinner, making sure that there was enough for me and Marvyn to eat now, plus Robyn and Rhyan if they came over later.

Honestly, I wasn't looking forward to seeing Rhyan again. She kept playing games, and with me being fresh out of a breakup, I didn't have time for it.

Why couldn't she get that?

She either wanted me or she didn't, and our time in Hopewellston proved to me that she didn't.

I sighed loudly as I continued chopping cabbage to make coleslaw.

Marvyn entered the kitchen. He raised a brow. "Wa yu in here a miserable up yuself 'bout?"

"Nothing," I lied.

"Hmm," Marvyn hummed. "Your mood wouldn't have anything to do with Rhyan, would it?" he asked, and I stiffened. "You're fucking her, aren't you?"

Realizing it made no sense to continue hiding it, I stopped chopping the cabbage. I leaned against the counter behind me as I looked at Marvyn, who had a knowing smirk on his face. "How do you know that?" I asked.

Marvyn scoffed. "I was your age once, you know? This isn't my first rodeo. I've been fucking before you were born."

Unfazed by Marvyn's blunt, inappropriate language, I shrugged. "I know.

That's how I got here."

He laughed. "Answer me."

"Yes," I said, and my shoulders felt lighter with the confession finally out in the air.

Marvyn grinned. "Everything's working out even better than I thought."

"What do you mean?" I asked as I went back to chopping.

"Rhyan hasn't told you about her dad?" he asked.

I shook my head. Rhyan never enjoyed speaking about her dad, so I did my best to avoid the topic as much as possible.

"Long story short..." Marvyn trailed off as he came further into the kitchen and sat atop a stool by the island. "He died in the Army. Robyn said she's been getting payouts for the Army since then — something about indemnity. I wasn't listening to all the details because I wasn't interested, but I do know that when I marry Robyn, I'll be able to have access to it."

My brows furrowed. I hadn't known that was how Rhyan lost her Dad. Why was Marvyn talking so carefree about it? He didn't even seem to have an ounce of pity for his future wife.

"Well, *we*," Marvyn added, correcting himself. "Because you can convince Rhyan to give you access to her share."

"*What*?" I asked, aghast. I must not have heard him correctly. No way Marvyn was suggesting what I thought he was.

"You heard me."

"Has this been what you've been doing all this time?" I asked, now remembering that his ex-spouses had once been military wives, and my sisters' moms were beneficiaries to inheritances. Horror filled my chest as I saw Marvyn in a new light that he'd done well to conceal.

My fucking father was a con-artist.

"Don't act surprised," Marvyn said coolly.

"I am! What the fuck!" I exclaimed. "I won't be a part of this."

His brows pulled together. The first real emotion came to his face — worry. "Kingston, I need you. If you leave suddenly and aren't at the wedding on Saturday, they'll suspect that something is wrong."

My jaw clenched tight. I'd spent all my life doing my best to not be a disappointment to Marvyn. He had daughters who hated him, friends who came and went, and family who wanted him nowhere near them.

But I'd always been here.

Because when my mother flew from Jamaica with me as a toddler and left me in Marvyn's arms, he didn't abandon me, too. He could've given me up for adoption. Could've begged Dallas' mom to raise me because she would've, so long as she got a cheque bigger than the one she already got on a monthly.

I never had a choice but to be by Marvyn's side, but when he was showing me his true colors, it wasn't a side that I wanted to be by.

Not anymore.

Without another word, I left all the ingredients atop the counter and went back to the room I was staying in. While I packed my things, Marvyn's voice came through the closed door.

"Please stay, Kingston," he begged. "At least until the wedding. After that, you can leave just like your sisters. I know you always wanted to."

I huffed and packed my belongings into the travel bag faster. I needed to be back in New Jersey as soon as possible.

No lie, I was going to miss Rhyan. But I didn't have the heart to drop by her place to tell her the truth about Marvyn's plans to rob Robyn.

Not that I owed her anything — she didn't want me anyway. But in honor of all the times we shared and all the moments we could've had, me leaving for good was the only way I could help her.

Chapter Nine

WHERE THERE'S A FIRE, ADD MORE FUEL

RHYAN

Loving my job was one thing, but when it had become my sole focus for almost a whole week? I was one inconvenience away from putting in my two-week notice. Dismissal was thirty minutes away, and three of my kids were in my office. One of them was doing their homework. Another had been napping. The other one was V-Logging on my phone.

I fussed with my bottom lip as I watched her. I couldn't believe I was about to do this, but the other two were too occupied to pay attention anyway. "Zayria," I said, and she stopped pretending to be an influencer to look at me.

"Yes, Miss Fagan?"

"Does your guardian pick you up after school?"

Her brows pulled together. "Which one? My brother or my mother?"

"Your, um, brother," I said before clearing my throat. Yup. I was definitely going to get fired if I didn't quit first.

She shook her head, a knowing smile on her lips. "No, but I can get him to—"

"No," I rushed out, and my other kid looked up from his homework to raise a brow at me.

"Is Zayria bothering you, Miss Fagan?" he asked.

"No," I said with a smile. "Finish up your work."

As he shifted his attention back to the work, Zayria looked at me. "Are you sure, Miss Fagan? It's no problem at all. He comes here all the time."

"I'm going to pretend I didn't hear that, Zayria," I said as I came to my senses.

"And let's just drop the entire conversation."

She nodded and started making another video.

A heavy sigh passed my lips as I looked down at the stack of papers on my desk. Chatter was drifting from the hallway from a few of my work colleagues and students.

I could hardly wait for the bell to ring. I needed weed badly, but me almost knowingly crossing a line with Zayria made me realize I needed to get a grip on myself.

My poisons were caffeine and alcohol. That shouldn't change due to my unease from not hearing from Kingston for a few days.

I devoted myself to my work until the bell finally rang, dismissing classes for the day. Zayria tapped her friend awake, then all three left my office. When they were gone, I lingered behind to help with ensuring students were going to their buses or private vehicles in an orderly fashion. Then, I went home.

I was soaking in the bathtub after a session with my vibrating dildo, which still rested within arm's length atop the toilet top, when Mom called me. "Hi, bestie," I greeted her with a smile.

"Hi!" she said, and I imagined her smiling. "I wanted to know if you were still coming over tonight to keep me company, or did you want me to come and get you tomorrow instead?"

"I'd said I would come over later tonight," I answered.

"Oh... I was just making sure. I know you tend to change your mind a lot, or I have to beg you to follow through with our plans."

I chuckled. "Mom, why would I miss spending the day with you before you get married? Addie helped me make the itinerary for Saturday. It's a full schedule, but I promise you'll be in bed before nine so you can look your best on your wedding day."

"Rhyan, you're making me teary eyed," she said, and I chuckled.

"I'll be over later, okay? I'm just taking some time to relax in my bathtub. Today was a long day at school. You know how these kids get on Fridays," I laughed, and she hummed.

"I'll leave you to it then. Let me know what time I should come and get you. I promise I'll be there on time."

"*Sure,*" I said sarcastically, making her gasp. "I'm just kidding, Mom..." I trailed off, then cleared my throat. "Hey, Mom?"

"Yes, baby?"

"Is Kingston okay?" I asked, desperate to know. I'd given him enough time to cool off after our return from Hopewellston. Saturday would be the last day we'd all be able to be together until the wedding on Sunday. There was no better time than then for us to come clean to our parents about our feelings for each other. It would either make or break Marvyn and Mom's wedding, but Kingston was right. We were all adults. Things would be awkward at first, but I trusted that if our parents truly wanted to see us happy, they would accept our relationship.

"I guess so. Why?"

My brows pulled together. "Why do you sound so unsure?"

Mom sighed. "Because I wish I could tell you. Marvyn has been a little on edge lately, and he's dodging my questions about Acheem, too."

I frowned. That knot resurfaced in my gut — the first time in the longest. It was tight with unease and uncertainty about Marvyn. "See you later, Mom," I said and ended the call before she could get another word in.

Something must've happened between Marvyn and Kingston. Maybe it was just a coincidence, but I didn't like the timing of things at all.

When I was a little girl, I'd always wished that I had been old enough to remember my parents' wedding when it had happened. I'd only ever seen photos around the house when I'd lived with Mom again.

As beautiful as she'd looked in her long, flowy white dress on that day, that was exactly how she looked now.

I smiled at her as I fixed the ornament in her hair that connected to her veil. Mom and I had straightened our curly hair. I'd even dyed mine back to black, just for this occasion.

My eyes filled with tears as I admired her. "Mom," I said, taking her gloved hands into mine. "You look so beautiful."

She smiled back at me. She was teary eyed, too. "Thank you, Rhyan. Stop it. You're going to make me cry, and I don't want to ruin my makeup."

"We'd never hear the end of it from Addie if we ruined it," I said with a laugh, making her chuckle. "Okay. You'll stay here and I'll go do another walk around to make sure everything's in place for when the ceremony begins."

Mom nodded as we freed our hands. She went to look at herself in the mirror and snap more pictures in addition to the ones we'd taken together already.

I left the room at the event center, then walked outside to the tent while fiddling with one of my favorite silver bracelets around my right wrist. The event organizer, someone Marvyn said was a friend who owed him a favor, did the decorations for free. Everything from the tablecloths to the fake flowers had a matching aesthetic of blue and white.

Mom and Marvyn's wedding was intended to be small and intimate. Outside of Mom's work colleagues, who I refused to greet, Addie, and people who introduced themselves as Marvyn's friends, there weren't many people here.

Which once again led me to the question I'd been asking myself since I came: where was Kingston?

He was supposed to be here. He promised. As much as the last time we saw each other, it wasn't on a good note, I doubted he would've let that come in the way of his father's wedding. Out of the four that he attended in the past, why would he not attend the fifth?

Something happened. I knew it, but I couldn't put a finger on what it was. The unease formed tight in my gut again, making me search the small gathering until my eyes landed on the source of my distress.

Marvyn was smiling brightly while speaking to a man.

How could he be so happy when Kingston wasn't here? Mom had said he'd been nervous all the days leading up to this moment, but she'd brushed it off as him being on edge about the wedding. Initially, I'd thought the same, but the warning bells were going off so loudly in my head now that I could no longer convince myself that Marvyn was truly the cookie-cutter image of the perfect man he claimed to be.

"Rhyan, are you alright?" Addie asked out of nowhere.

I startled in surprise. My attention unwillingly dragged from Marvyn to Addie. She stood by my side, one hand on my arm while her eyes, full of concern, raked all over me.

"Yes," I said and loosened my fists that I hadn't realized had tightened. "Stall the wedding."

"Huh?" Addie asked, her brows pulling together.

"Stall the wedding," I said firmly. "I need to talk to Mom. Something's not right."

I could practically see the wheels turning in Addie's head as she nodded. While she went off somewhere, I went back to the private rooms.

Mom spun around as I entered the room. The smile faded from her face as she saw my expression, and concern filled her eyes. "Rhyan? What's wrong?"

"Where's Kingston?" I asked her, lingering by the door.

"He's still not here?" Mom asked, and I shook my head. "Weird… Maybe he's back in Jersey, though I can't understand why…"

"Something's wrong, Mom."

"How so?" she asked. "Talk to me."

I sucked in a breath. "I think you should have a seat. I have a lot to tell you."

"No, Rhyan," Mom said firmly. She crossed her arms beneath her bust. "What's wrong? Talk to me *now*. Today isn't the day for you to—"

"I'm having sex with Kingston," I blurted.

Mom paused.

Her mouth dropped.

She blinked once.

Twice.

Then, her mouth snapped shut, and she walked toward the nearest chair. She plopped down into it. "W-What?" she asked, her voice lower than a whisper.

I sighed. With the secret off my shoulder, I felt so much lighter. "Yes, Mom," I said. I took a step forward, but she held up a finger, signaling me to stay right where I was. That was warranted, but I was still a little hurt. "It happened before we knew about you and Marvyn."

"The cruise?" she asked, and I nodded. "And when you came back, were you still?"

"Yes, Mom," I said. I felt like a little girl all over again.

Right then, I had a vivid memory of the day I'd been playing around in her bedroom and accidentally bounced a picture frame off her dresser. It had shattered into tens of pieces. Trying to hide the damage with tape and glue was pointless. Left with no choice, I gathered the pieces into my hands and went to Mom with tears in my eyes, on edge because I didn't know if she would scold me or help me put the pieces back together.

"I know how messed up it is, but you have to believe me when I say that none of us intended for this to happen," I added.

"Rhyan... I don't know what to say."

I took a step forward. She didn't stop me, so I took another and another until I was before her. As I sat on the chair next to hers, I said, "You don't have to say anything. Not right now. Just listen. Something is up with Marvyn."

"Are you saying this so I can break up with Marvyn and you can get to be with Kingston, or are you telling me the truth?"

"The truth, Mom. I've never lied to you," I said, and she pursed her lips, knowing that was true. "Since the first day I met Marvyn, I had a gut feeling something was wrong with him. Did I tell you that when we were at the restaurant, I bumped into him by the restroom, and his wallet fell from his hands? He had a stack of cards that all had different names—" I gasped. My eyes widened as I held Mom's stare. "I think he's a scammer. A con-artist. Something that's the opposite of who he claims to be. That's why he's in such a hurry to get married. He wants access to your money."

Mom's mouth fell. She went quiet for a moment while I held my breath. Then, an emotion flashed across her face. Was it realization or something else? I couldn't tell. All I knew was that she stood, hands clenched at her sides, then she walked out of the room.

I followed closely behind her. Watched as she stopped before Marvyn, who seemed surprised to see her for more reasons than one.

"Robyn—" he began, and Mom slapped his words back into his mouth.

The crowd gasped.

I smirked.

Marvyn's eyes met mine. The collected expression I was so used to seeing from him was gone. His eyes burned with anger.

I grinned.

Now that that was over, I needed to go to New Jersey to get my man, or slap him like Mom did his father — just for him thinking that he could just up and leave without a word.

But first, I needed to go see where that sudden smell of something burning was coming from. I was pretty sure that Addie had started a fire somewhere.

Chapter Ten

WHERE THERE'S AN ENDING, TURN IT INTO A NEW BEGINNING

KINGSTON

Tim snatched up the container of dried fruits, holding it at a distance away from me. "Acheem," he started.

"Oh, brother," I said, mimicking his voice and causing him to chuckle.

"Mockery's the highest form of flattery," he said.

My brow's furrowed. "I thought it was imitation?"

"Besides the point," Tim said as he placed the container back onto the counter. He kept his hand close to it, ready to snatch it away again if I reached for it.

Shaking my head at Tim's antics, I looked back at the charcuterie board laid out before me. It was still in progress, almost finished, so I could move on to the next. Escargot had a last minute addition to the reservations — someone who was an old friend of Tim's — and the restaurant was swamped. That was how Tim finally called me in. Yet, he kept hovering over me and constantly came back into the kitchen to remind me that I was still on vacation, and he'd be sending me home as soon as the rush was over.

"You've been working like a horse since you came back," Tim said, as I expected. "Relax."

"No. I rested enough in Jamaica and Florida," I said to Tim, hoping he would drop it. If he sent me home earlier than expected tonight, I'd start searching for new charcuterie jobs by morning.

I needed to work.

Distract my mind.

Stop worrying about whether Robyn had signed those marriage papers earlier today and allowed Marvyn to fuck over her and Rhyan.

"Alright," Tim said, realizing I wasn't in the mood to entertain him. He slid the container toward me, and I stopped it with my hand. "But don't think I'm calling you in tomorrow."

RHYAN

I took hurried steps through the airport, still in my heels and bridesmaid dress. People gave me awkward glances, but I ignored them all. Of all the crazy things I heard happened in New Jersey, people had no right side eyeing a girl from Florida.

Addie had tried getting me to change into something more comfortable for the near three hour flight, but I refused. It was imperative for me to get to Jersey as soon as possible. Literally a life or death situation.

Well, I was just being dramatic as always, but I really needed to be there quickly.

I wasn't sure where in this big city Kingston lived, but I knew he worked at a restaurant called Escargot. My plan was to go there, and then...

Then, what?

Well, I hadn't thought that through clearly.

I'd just been winging it for the entire day.

I tightened my grip on the strap of the bag thrown over my shoulder, ensuring I wouldn't lose my wallet with all of my money, IDs, phone, and passport. Outside, I asked someone for instructions toward a taxi stand. When I got there, I hopped into the first one and told them to bring me to Escargot.

Staring through the window for the entire journey made me appreciate the views. Where I lived in Jacksonville didn't have anywhere near this many high-rise buildings. It was somewhat intimidating, yet beautiful at the same time.

I truly loved seeing new places.

The driver parked at the curb before the restaurant, and I gave him the fare plus a tip. I exited the vehicle and stood outside. From the outside, the restaurant didn't seem too busy. Still, that might've been because it was only five in the evening.

Inhaling a breath to steady my racing heart, I held it for a moment before releasing it. My steps were unsteady as I entered the establishment, the smell of delicious meals and the low ambiance lights greeting me as I approached the hostess stand.

"Good afternoon," greeted the host. Her eyes held much curiosity about my choice of outfit.

Okay. Next time, before choosing to impulsively do something, I was definitely going to take a moment to change my outfit. My feet were starting to hurt from running around in these heels and almost breaking my ankles on several occasions, plus all the unwanted attention was making me uncomfortable.

"Good afternoon," I answered, giving her my best smile. "Does Kingston Badalo work here?" I asked, now worried that his falling off the map included him getting a new job elsewhere.

Her smile didn't waver. "I'm sorry. I'm not allowed to give out employee information."

"Please," I said, ready to cry if I must. "I traveled all the way from Florida. I'm really tired, my ankles are swollen, and it's been a very long day. I have to talk to him. *Please*. Tell him it's Rhyan."

She pursed her lips. Worry creased her face as she continued to stare me down.

Finally, she relaxed. She nodded at me and pointed toward a bench in the waiting area. While she disappeared further into the restaurant, I had a seat. I rested my bag on my lap and leaned forward to rub at my ankles.

I sensed Kingston before I saw him.

His cologne fogged all my senses. His tall stature blocked the light from shining on me.

My breath caught in my throat. I was scared to lift my head and see the man who had caused me unrest for the past week, but I had to put on my big girl panties. Stop being childish, as he'd claimed I was being.

Swallowing to dampen my suddenly dry throat, I looked up.

There he was.

Kingston Badalo.

The man with the perfect white teeth smile, dark skin that greatly complemented mine, and the well-groomed goatee and beard, paired with a nice trim. He was in a chef's jacket.

His eyes never left mine. They were void of emotion. He didn't look happy to see me. Didn't convey if he knew what his father's plans were for my family.

Hesitantly, I rose to my feet. "Hi," I said, my voice low.

"Rhyan," he said, making me shiver. Not because my body got excited at him saying my name for the first time in however long. But because even his tone was cold. As if I wasn't the same woman who he'd spent an unforgettable cruise with and constantly begged to be in a relationship with.

I wouldn't let it faze me though. I deserved this — his anger, his dismissal, all his emotions.

"Is there somewhere private we could talk?" I asked.

"No."

"Okay…" So he just wanted to get straight to the point and skip all salutations? Fine. I cleared my throat. "Did you know about Marvyn?" I asked, and there it was.

Kingston's first inkling of emotion.

His eyes flashed concern. Regret. Shame.

"No," he admitted with a slight shake of his head. "I'm sorry. I know I should've said something, but." He paused and released a ragged breath. "I didn't know how."

"Okay," I said, knowing the earnestness in his voice and on his face couldn't be faked. "I'm glad you didn't. Because I'd hate to have to call the police and get you arrested, too."

"Marvyn's in jail?"

I nodded. "Being processed as we speak."

Kingston sighed. He moved to sit on the bench. I didn't like looking down at him, so I sat beside him. I was scared to touch him, but I hoped my presence was enough to alleviate some of the weight that appeared on his shoulders.

"I'm sorry, Rhyan," he said again, then kept repeating it over and over.

"Hey." I laid my hand atop his thigh, cutting off his rambling. "It's okay. You didn't know. And that's what makes you better than him. Don't feel bad about it. I won't hold it over your head because nothing happened."

Kingston stopped looking down at the floor to finally meet my eyes. Kingston looked... soft. The opposite of the cold man who greeted me. He was wearing his heart on his sleeve, right before my eyes, and I hoped he'd let me take it into my hold again.

"That's not the only reason why I'm here," I said, and his brow raised. "I'm here for us. If you still want me, that is."

"You told Robyn?" he asked, making me nod. "And?"

"And what?"

"She's accepting us?"

I shrugged. "I'm not sure, but it doesn't matter what Mom wants. I know what I want. And that's you. Here in Jersey, or anywhere else. Please forgive me for how I went about things. I hadn't realized how I was hurting you by playing around when you were fresh out of a relationship. I'm sorry, Kingston."

A moment passed.

Kingston said nothing.

I held my breath.

From the corner of my eye, I saw the hostess blatantly listening in on our conversation while low music and chatter from diners filled the silence between us.

Just when my skin was beginning to turn red, and I was sure that I'd die from the lack of oxygen, Kingston spoke.

"Okay," he said.

My mouth dropped. "*Okay*?" I repeated with my brows pulled together. I yanked my hand back to my lap as if his skin had the plague. "That's all you have to say?"

"What else do you want me to say, Rhyan?"

"*Anything* except that," I hissed. "Tell me how you feel. Tell me that you want me. Or don't want me—"

"I want you, Rhyan," Kingston cut me off. "Always."

My jaw clenched tight. Had Kingston flipped the script and was playing jokes with me now? "It doesn't seem like it," I said, angry as I stood. God, I was such an idiot. As I was about to walk away, Kingston grabbed my wrist. His grip was tight as I stared up at his infuriatingly handsome face.

"Damn, shorty. I can't take a moment to process that I have no parents now?" he asked, and I halted in my tracks.

There I went again. Jumping to conclusions when it came to this man. I wasn't usually like this — I studied Psychology, for crying out loud — but I'd never been open to being in a relationship like this before him, either.

"I'm sorry," I rushed out, cupping my yappy mouth with my free hand.

He chuckled. The light returned to his eyes. He stared at me with such admiration that my red skin wasn't from anger or embarrassment, but from how hard I was blushing. "We'll work on that attitude of yours when I come home tonight."

"Tonight?" I squeaked.

He nodded. "You think I'd let you come all this way just to send you back to Florida?"

"Well..."

"Rhyan," he laughed before moving my hand from my mouth. His head swooped down, and his mouth captured mine.

My eyes fluttered closed. Kingston wrapped an arm around my waist, tugging me closer. My chest pressed against his body as he kissed me hard. This heated kiss was a public claim, a declaration for us to stand together and face whatever conflicts may arise from us being together.

Teeth clashing, we kissed like we were hungry.

Starving.

Beyond insatiable for each other.

The world faded around us as I smiled into the kiss.

In the moment, nothing else mattered except him.

Me.

Us.

A forever one life stand.

Glossary

Me tell you don' call me Daddy. Me name Marvyn. Daddy a fi batty man, and if me was a batty man, me wouldn' have you or the ungrateful one dem. | I told you not to call me Daddy. My name's Marvyn. Gay men are called 'daddy', and if I was a gay man, I wouldn't have you or your ungrateful siblings.

See the bwoy deh | There he is

Wah'm to yu | What's wrong with you

Big up yuself | Take care of yourself

Yu know say you a problem | You know that you're trouble

Wa yu in here a miserable up yuself 'bout | Why're you in here being miserable

Also by J.B. Stephens

All for You: *A Why Choose Romance*
Trial of Deceit: The Family's Oath #1: *A Dark Romance*
Taeja: *A Why Choose Romance*
The Crossfire: *A Dark Romance*

As Adajay Brown

Fall Out: All that Glitters #2: *A Coming-of-Age Novel*
Bruk Out: All that Glitters #1: *A Coming-of-Age Novel*

About the Author

J.B. Stephens is a Jamaican who enjoys creating worlds with words. She hopes to hook readers from the first page, then carry them along an emotional journey — whether it be swooning at something romantic or sexy a character said, or crying because she is a word wizard with the ability to summon raw emotions through her work.

She also writes young adult as Adajay Brown.

When she's not daydreaming about her ever-growing fictional world, which she's dubbed "ADALAND", J.B. can be found binge-watching police procedurals and supernatural series, getting lost in fantasy, romance, or thriller novels, eating white chocolate, or connecting with readers through her social media platforms.

To stay in touch with J.B. Stephens, visit: authorjbstephens.com

www.ingramcontent.com/pod-product-compliance
Lightning Source LLC
LaVergne TN
LVHW050319160826
845677LV00014B/3472

* 9 7 9 8 9 9 5 0 5 0 1 1 7 *